Capturing a Diamond

SEALed for You

* Ace in the Hole
* Explosive Passion

Marissa Dobson

Published by Sunshine Press
Printed in the United States of America
ISBN: 978-1-939978-45-5

Dedication

To all the men and woman in the military who serve our country, and their families.

Capturing a Diamond – SEALed for You

Contents

Capturing a Diamond – SEALed for You

Ace in the Hole

SEALed for You:
Book One

Capturing a Diamond – SEALed for You

Ace Diamond left behind the woman he loved when he joined the Navy SEALs. For years he focused on his career, risking life and limb on missions for his country. Now home on leave, he must face his past and ask himself if leaving her was a mistake.

At seventeen, Gwyneth London gave her heart away only to have it broken. More than a dozen years later, she decides to embrace her single life and have a child on her own. Ready to start over in her hometown, she doesn't expect to see the man who still holds her heart, but when he walks back into her life she's unable to push him away.

Can Gwyneth and Ace claim the life they were supposed to have, or will they let love pass them by?

Capturing a Diamond – SEALed for You

Chapter One

Ace Diamond tossed his duffle bag at the foot of the steps and admired the peaceful sanctuary he called home. The old Victorian house he was born and raised in was now his. Since purchasing it from his parents after they decided to buy an RV and travel the country, very little had changed. Family photos lined the wide staircase; everything was well used and loved, none of that stuffiness some old houses had. The memories of his childhood played out everywhere he looked.

He'd made it home after months of blood, death, and war that had taken a toll on his body and his spirit. He needed a break, not to mention a week's worth of sleep.

This deployment had been harder than any of the others. Too many of his fellow warriors had been killed. Memories of the bloodshed haunted him every time he closed his eyes. Too many recollections he would have rather left behind. He was a different man than when he left a year ago, and he could no longer look at the world the same way. Everywhere he looked he saw people taking freedom for granted. So many of them didn't even realize that more men and women than he'd care to count gave their lives for those freedoms. This deployment served to remind him just how expensive that freedom was.

Dishes clattered in the kitchen, drawing him from his thoughts and back to the present.

"Wynn?" He made his way toward the large farmhouse kitchen in the rear. Coming around the corner, he expected to find his little sister. Instead, he saw a woman with a short pixie haircut, red hair sticking up every which way, holding a knife in her hand.

"Who are you?" Fear coated her voice.

He looked at the small knife, knowing it would be easy to disarm her if he had to. "Better question is who are you? After all, you're in my house."

"Ace…" Her eyes widened in surprise. "You're not supposed to be here. Wynn said you wouldn't be back for a couple more weeks."

"Well, I'm here, so why don't you tell me who you are?" He leaned against the wide entryway into the kitchen, crossing his arms over his chest.

"Gwen." With a shaky hand, she set the knife on the counter. "Wynn told me I could stay here until I found a place of my own. I came back for my mother's funeral and couldn't leave. You don't realize how much you miss home until you come back."

"Gwyneth London, it can't be." He took in the woman before him. *Wow!*

"You didn't recognize me at first, so I thought maybe you forgot all about me."

"You look so different." Different was an understatement. Her long blonde hair had been replaced with the red spiky do, and she had developed curves in all the right places. She was gorgeous. Gathering himself together, he nodded. "I'm sorry about your mom. She was an amazing woman."

"Thank you." She leaned against the counter. "I was making a sandwich. Can I make you one?"

"No thanks, I grabbed something on my way home from the airport, but go ahead." She turned back to the cutting board and cut into the turkey, tomato, and lettuce sandwich. That was when he saw the slight protruding tummy, the beginnings of the curve of pregnancy. Was she?

"You noticed." Sometime while he was lost in his thoughts she turned around, sandwich in one hand, her other hand resting on the curve of her stomach.

"Are you…?"

"Pregnant? Yes."

"Is that the reason you decided to stay?"

"Let's sit, I'll explain while I eat." She moved past him into the dining room, and took a seat at the head of the long dining table. She took a bite out of the sandwich before meeting his gaze. "For years

I've been so focused on my career, never sparing time for a personal life, let alone dating or even thinking of children."

"Then how?"

"Two years ago I was in a car accident and was in a coma for weeks. When I woke, I realized there was so much more in life. More that I wanted." She ran her hand over her stomach. "Four months ago I decided I wanted to start a family. So I went to a fertility clinic, and well...you can see the results."

"Why not do it the old-fashioned way?" His eyes widened, appalled that she let a doctor impregnate her instead of doing it the way their parents had.

"To do it that way, you need a man. One-night stands tend to get upset when you use them to have a child without telling them. This seemed a better route."

"But you'll be doing it all on your own. No father to help raise the child."

"I can raise a child myself. My mother practically did it with me and I turned out just fine. The important part is there's no father to try to take my child away."

She polished off the rest of her sandwich while he sat there trying to figure out what to say to that. Gwen had never been the average woman. No, she had been strong, and full of life. She'd never let a man or anyone tell her what to do.

"I realize you don't agree..."

"What makes you say that?" He didn't like that she found him so easy to read.

"We might have been out of touch for years, but I know you, Ace Le Diamond. I can see the disappointment in your pretty blue eyes. You were raised in a perfect family by both parents. I wasn't so lucky, and my child won't be either, but she'll never lack for anything. Please don't disrespect my decision just because you don't agree with it."

"Wow." He held up his hands in front of him, warding off her answer. "I said nothing and did nothing to disrespect your decision. I was only thinking back to when we were kids. You always said you wanted a husband, two and a half kids, a dog, and a house with a white picket fence. All these years that I haven't seen you, I just figured you found what you wanted."

He kept it to himself that even though Wynn stayed in touch with her, he deliberately lost touch. The attraction between them had always been strong, drawing them together through everything, but when he joined the military, the distance began, only to worsen when he made the SEAL team. She might have been proud of him, but the fear that lingered in her eyes tore at his heart. Distance seemed to be the only way to avoid it.

He had never wanted to cause her any pain, and seeing it there in her eyes he knew the only way to change it was to step back. To let their friendship drift away until she no longer cared about him. It was hard, and over the years he had thought about her, but giving up his career as a SEAL wasn't an option. He was meant for the excitement and the thrill. It was everything he was.

Capturing a Diamond – SEALed for You

Chapter Two

Gwen couldn't believe Ace was there, sitting beside her. The man who'd stolen her heart, the man who still had it but had no idea. So much time had passed since they'd seen each other, and there he sat looking like not a single day had gone by. Her heart sped, her palms were sweaty, and she felt lightheaded just being near him again. She hated that he had such an effect on her.

She took a sip of the milk she had brought in with her sandwich. "I'll call my realtor and see if she can find me a short term apartment to rent while I'm house searching. If not, I can get a hotel room."

"There's no reason to do that. My mission ended early but I've been reassigned to a training mission. I leave in three days, so you might as well stay put."

"I don't want to be in your way." Nor was she sure she wanted to be alone with him for three days when she couldn't seem to get control of her emotions now.

"You won't be, but if it becomes an issue for either of us I can bunk at Wynn's. I'm assuming you took over the master bedroom, so I'll stay in the guest room."

"Guest room? You mean the storage area." She teased, giving her something to say besides the fact that she took his bedroom to be close to him. It sounded stupid, especially since she hadn't seen him in years, but being in his house, it brought back all the old feelings she buried deep within her.

"When I bought the house from Mom and Dad, I was leaving for a deployment. I barely had time to get my stuff from my condo and bring it over here. Since then, it's just kind of piled up in that room. I keep hoping one day between deployments I'll be able to deal with it, make room for it or just get rid of it, but it never happens."

"Wynn said you're never here, she can't figure out why you wanted this place anyway."

"It's home. It might sound cheesy but if ever the day comes when I can have a family of my own, I want them here. I want the pictures that line the staircase to be of my children and family, to have them enjoy the treehouse my father and I built when I was a kid. Silly, right?"

"No." She shook her head, wishing she could do the same with her child. For that, she'd have to have a place she considered home. Instead, she was going to find a cute little house on the edge of town, with a little land that her daughter could play in.

"It doesn't matter how long I'm gone, when I walk through the front door I feel like I'm at home. I never had that with my condo. Plus, I couldn't picture someone else living in this house. It's the Diamond household, and since Wynn wasn't going to move out of her beach condo, I bought it."

The Diamond household.

Oh, she knew what that meant. It was so much more than just a name. They'd had some amazing parties in this house, and had a tendency to do it Vegas style. Not hard to believe since Mrs. Diamond had named her kids for their poker party days. The Diamonds weren't gamblers, they preferred playing for favors or candy. Nothing illegal, but they played it like it was all or nothing. No one who knew them was surprised when she named the children Ace, Lucky, and Wynn.

The silence ticked by until he finally spoke. "Moving back here, what about your career?"

"I'm a virtual legal researcher, so it can be done anywhere there's internet. Plus, the company I work for has a second branch in downtown Virginia Beach, so if I ever need to go into the office, there's one close."

"Where were you before?"

"Nashville, Tennessee, that's where the main branch of Madison and Strine is. They hired me fresh out of college."

"What did they have to say about…your pregnancy?"

"They only know I'm pregnant, not how." She ran her hand over the curve of her stomach. "I paid for everything off the books, didn't use my insurance for any of it. Not because I'm embarrassed by my choice, but because it was no one's business."

"Instead your employer thinks you've slept around."

She shot to her feet. "How dare you!"

"I apologize, that was out of line." Remorse was clear on his face.

"Damn right it was. You have no right to judge me."

"Gwen, I'm sorry, I just wasn't thinking. This all came as a shock. I never expected you to go about it the way you have."

"I've changed from the little girl you used to know." She grabbed the plate and glass from the table. "There's a lot that happened over the years that would shock you. Maybe if you would have stayed in touch you'd know." She stormed off into the kitchen before the tears came.

One of the things she hated most about being pregnant was the tears. She hated being so emotionally uncertain. She could cry at any moment, and the next she'd be laughing as if nothing happened. *Hormones.*

The soles of his boots echoed on the hardwood floor as he followed her. "Listen, Gwen, I am really sorry. I know it doesn't change anything, but I am."

"You're right, it doesn't. Sorry doesn't fix anything, it doesn't mend hurt feelings." She placed the dishes in the dishwasher and started cleaning up the counter without looking at him.

He leaned against the island behind her, and kept his words low as if he wasn't sure she should hear him. "All these years I hoped you had found a wonderful man and had that perfect family you always wanted."

Pain shot through her heart. "You never bothered to ask Wynn what happened? Every time we talked I made sure to ask about you."

"No." It came out in a low whisper. She wasn't sure he'd spoken until she turned around and saw him shaking his head. "I didn't…I had hoped if I left things be, then you would be able to find someone to give you everything you deserved. We both know I wasn't the one to give you what you wanted."

"You *chose* to not be that person, without even giving me a say in it." She didn't bother to wipe away the tears that were freely falling down her cheeks. "What did you think would happen? That I'd just forget about you, the time we shared together, and find someone new? Do you really think I'm that much of a bitch?"

"I never said that. Damn it, Gwen, I did what I thought was right." He slapped his hand on the counter.

"Here I thought I always had a say in what was right for me." She threw the dishrag in the sink. "Just forget it."

Capturing a Diamond – SEALed for You

Chapter Three

Shocked and unable to believe how quickly things had gotten out of hand, Ace just stood there watching Gwen stalk from the kitchen. She was upset, tears streaming down her face, and he wasn't sure how to make anything better. When he put distance between them, he did it for her. It hadn't been easy for him, but neither was seeing her again.

He wanted to believe that all those years ago, he had made the right decision, that he wasn't the reason she was single and pregnant now, but for the first time he had some serious doubt. Seeing her there in his family home brought back all the memories, bringing to life all the feelings he had for her.

Every part of him itched to go after her, to comfort her. Instead, he kept himself rooted to the spot. Feeling her in his arms would be the end of him. He'd never be able to stuff his emotions and hide them away again. Before he realized it, he was halfway across the open space, nearing the steps.

"Get it together, Diamond." With one last glare at the steps, he forced himself to turn away from them. He'd get himself under control and then go upstairs and get some rest.

In three days, he'd be leaving again. He couldn't forget his life revolved around training and missions, there was nothing left over for a committed relationship. Gwen needed a man who would be there, and now she needed a father for her child. He couldn't be that, and thinking otherwise wasn't fair to her.

His cell phone rang, pulling him back from the brink of his dangerous thoughts. He snatched it from the table and checked the caller ID.

Rebel. What trouble is he getting into now?

Luke "Rebel" Rodríguez wasn't that much younger then Ace, but he partied like he was still twenty-one. Wherever he went he managed to find trouble. It didn't matter where he was or what he was doing, trouble followed him around like a shadow.

He slid his finger across the screen, and brought it to his ear. "I thought you'd be catching up on your sleep so you could get crazy tonight."

"I'm about to do just that. I'm surprised you're not already asleep. Diamond, with your old age, you need your rest. The guys and I are going out tonight, hitting this new club downtown. You coming?"

"No man, I already promised Wynn I'd stop over tonight." The excuse slipped out before he could stop himself. They had barely been off duty for a couple of hours and already Rebel was looking for fun. This time Ace wanted nothing to do with it. He wanted to stay home and maybe find a way to make up his blunder to Gwen.

"Come on, old man. You can do that early, then meet us for drinks."

"Next time, you have my word. Have a good time."

"Damn man, you and Boom are getting too old for your own good. Successful missions should be celebrated, you never know when the next one might be our last."

Wasn't that the truth, but not tonight.

"Boom?" He and Jared "Boom" Taylor were in the same SEAL class, going through the torture of training together. Sticking together, they'd somehow made it through when most of their class dropped out.

"Yeah, he's staying home tonight too. Something about a list of shit to do before we leave again."

He didn't like the fact that the boys were going out without him or Boom; they were the ones that kept the younger men in line and out of jail. "What's the name of the club?"

"Pulse. It's off Mediterranean Avenue, just past the Japanese restaurant. You can't miss the signs. Does that mean you're coming then?"

"I might stop by." He left it open, so if he didn't feel like going no one would be watching out for him.

"See you there." Excitement poured from Rebel's voice.

"Maybe," he reminded him before ending the call.

Just what I want to do, go out to a loud club. Don't the boys believe in resting at all?

With a shower calling to him, he slid the phone into his pocket, grabbed his olive top load canvas duffel bag and headed upstairs. Shower, some sleep, and then hopefully he'd have an idea how to fix the tension between Gwen and him without getting to close to her.

Gwen curled up on the king size bed. The tears had finally begun to subside when the shower kicked on in the hall bathroom. She had debated leaving. At this time of year, she could find a hotel without a problem, but something kept her there. Seeing Ace brought everything back with a vengeance. It broke her heart to hear the only man she ever loved stand there and criticize her choices.

It took a near fatal car accident to make her realize she couldn't keep waiting for him. She had to move on with her life. She fell in love with Ace in high school and never got over it. Even the few short-term boyfriends she'd had since then could never compare to him.

She'd once believed they would spend their lives together, though she hadn't been comfortable with the idea of being a military wife. That was where his ambition was, and she had accepted that. Then he just went off to boot camp and never looked back.

She didn't understand how he could just leave her without explaining it to her. All she received was a Dear Jane letter. She had hoped to be able to talk some sense into him, to get him to see reason, but every letter she wrote went unanswered. Finally, she decided to wait until he came back, but each time he had a break in his training he made an excuse. By the time he finished his training and joined SEAL team two, she had moved to Tennessee and was busy with her own career. Too much time had passed for her to seek him out; there was no logic left, only pain.

Sliding her hand along the curve of her stomach, her thoughts turned to her unborn daughter, and she tried to convince herself everything had worked out fine. Maybe not the way she wanted them to, but that didn't matter anymore. Now she had to focus on making a life for her and her daughter, and the first step was to find a new place to live.

Capturing a Diamond – SEALed for You

Chapter Four

Two houses down, Gwen and her realtor stood outside a condo building. The building was two blocks from the beach and just down the road from Wynn's. It was at the top end of her budget, but still within it if it didn't need a lot of work.

"This condo has two bedrooms, two baths, and the open floor plan you asked for. It also has a den you could use as your office." Trudy read off the house details while Gwen looked over the outside.

"What floor?"

"The eighth floor. There's a large balcony with nice views, as well as a play set on the other side of the building for the children. There's an indoor pool and fitness area, a large area on the first floor that can be used for birthday parties, events, pretty much anything a tenant needs. Shall we go inside?"

She nodded and followed her realtor to the door. The additional amenities the condo provided were appealing. So far, the only thing that wasn't was the additional housing fees associated with it.

"I know it wasn't entirely what you were looking for but I think it might work better for you. The building next door has a daycare in it that a lot of the families who live here use. The beach and almost everything you need is all within walking distance."

Another couple of positives for the condo that she added to her mental list. At this point, she didn't plan to use daycare. Her hours were flexible enough that it wasn't needed. She could always hire a daytime nanny if she needed someone to watch her daughter while she worked. That would allow her daughter to be home with her instead of in a daycare.

Inside, the creamy white marble tile and warm gold walls gave the place a touch of class. A small coffee area sat cattycorner to the door, with the television overhead tuned into one of the daytime soaps. It felt welcoming, almost as if it wasn't a lobby.

"There is security detail round the clock, they make sure there is fresh coffee out here at all times," Trudy explained, winking.

"Security?"

"There's nothing to worry about. There are never any issues, they're here as a precaution. So close to the beach, many of the condo owners are not year round residents, so the condo board decided it would put many of the owners at ease to have the security on site." Trudy pushed the up button in front of the bank of elevators.

The elevator doors opened and Lucky was standing there, Ace's younger brother. "Gwen? I can't believe it! That's you, isn't it?"

"Oh, Lucky, how nice it is to see you." She stepped into the elevator and wrapped her arms around him. "It's been too long."

"Tell me about it. What are you doing here?" His arms tightened around her until she couldn't breathe before finally letting her go. "You're pregnant."

Not having any desire to get into her pregnancy in front of Trudy, she nodded and quickly made introductions. "Lucky Diamond, this is my realtor Trudy, she's showing me a condo on the eighth floor."

"Condo eight-twelve."

"How did you know?"

"I'm next door in eight-eleven. A fellow Marine lived there, until he received his PCS." As if he realized at the last moment he was talking to a civilian, he added, "Permanent Change of Station."

"Hmm, we could be neighbors."

"Mind if I tag along, then maybe we could get some coffee and catch up?"

She nodded and realized the elevator doors had closed but they hadn't moved. "Sure, if you weren't off to do something."

"It can wait." He reached past Trudy and pushed the button for the eighth floor.

Gwen leaned against the wall between them, almost unable to believe it was Lucky standing in front of her. The sweet, slightly geeky boy from high school had grown into one fine looking man.

Being a Marine had given him muscles he didn't have before, and the shaggy hair had been replaced with a crew cut. He was attractive, but to her he was like a younger brother, nothing more. *At least he's happy to see me.*

Twenty minutes later the tour was complete and Gwen sat in Lucky's condo. The floor plan was identical to the one she'd just seen, the only difference was it was clear a single man lived here. Where a dining table should have been there was an air hockey table in its place, and there were weights near the television. Otherwise, the area was relatively spotless, not that she expected anything less from Lucky. He had always been the most organized of the Diamond family, and lived a strict timetable, making him a good fit for military life.

"So…" He leaned against the kitchen bar, watching her.

Knowing Lucky wouldn't come straight out with what was on his mind, she took a sip of the water and decided to cut to the point. "Did Wynn tell you, or are you wondering where my husband is?"

"She only told me you've moved back into town *alone*." He sat his beer down on the counter and gave her a serious look. "Do I need to break some guy's legs?"

With a lighthearted laugh, she realized how much she'd missed Lucky. He always could make her laugh, even when she thought her world was falling apart.

She laid her hand over his. "It's nothing like that. I did this on my own. It was time I had a family. My daughter was conceived by a sperm donor."

"Good for you." He laid his other hand on top of theirs giving it a squeeze. "You took your life in your own hands and got what you wanted. I'm sorry it wasn't how you pictured it, but you're living life on your own terms and there's nothing better than that."

His words sent a shockwave rippling through her. Even Wynn hadn't been supportive at first.

"Thank you. It means a lot to hear you say that."

"I know Ace is back in town and you were staying at the house while you searched for a place of your own, so if you need a place to stay you're welcome here. I have a guest room you can use."

"Thank you, Lucky, but it's not necessary." As she sipped her water, she pictured Ace's reaction to that. He would blow a gasket if he knew she was leaving his place to stay with his younger brother.

"I know how things went down with you two and I don't want you getting hurt again. It would be wrong if I have to beat the shit out of my own brother *again*. I'm not sure Mom would like that too much." He took a deep swig from his beer and watched her.

"I don't think Mrs. Diamond would be happy over her grown sons fighting, plus it's not worth it."

"You're worth it. Never doubt that."

"It's all in the past and that's where it's going to stay. I didn't decided to stay in town to be close to Ace, but because I have so many fond memories here. It's where I want my daughter to be raised."

In reality, when she'd decided to move back home, she had hoped she wouldn't bump into Ace. Her heart didn't need the pain. Too much time had passed for them to go back to the way things were, and the child growing inside her needed her to be at her best, not love sick over someone who'd left her without an explanation. Despite this, she couldn't get Ace out of her mind no matter how hard she tried.

Chapter Five

Adding the last of the chopped up potatoes and vegetables to the roaster, Ace slipped it into the oven. A nice pot roast with all the fixings just like his mother used to make. It was comfort food, always reminding him of his childhood. He hoped cooking for Gwen would help erase the unease from earlier.

He glanced at the clock and mentally noted the roast would be done in an hour. Hopefully, Gwen would make it back in time from wherever she'd disappeared to. Otherwise, he'd made the meal for himself. As much as he enjoyed it, if he was eating alone he would have rather gone out.

Later on, a slight creak told him the front door had opened and the clicking of heels followed. He grabbed the dishtowel and wiped his hands.

"Gwen?"

"Something smells good."

"Mom's famous pot roast recipe, or at least as near as I can get. I was hoping you'd join me for dinner, unless you have other plans." He stood by the kitchen bar, uneasy.

Sinking down onto the sofa, she dropped her purse on the coffee table and with a moan tugged off her heels. "Sorry, my feet were killing me."

"You were never much for heels. I think you were the only girl that went to our prom in flats." The memory of her prom dress tight around her curves made his shaft harden.

"I'd remind you those black ballet flats made the outfit." She smirked, rubbing the arch of her foot. "You wouldn't have wanted me to go with those sky high heels that were so popular then, and hear me moan all night about my sore feet. It would have put a damper on our fun."

"I wouldn't have changed anything about that night." He'd only change the stuff after that happened afterward.

She nibbled her bottom lip, something she always did when she was nervous, and changed the subject. "I'd have cooked when I got back."

"There's nothing to do but wait."

She leaned back on the sofa, watching him. "I figured you'd be sleeping for a while or I'd have left a note to tell you I had an appointment with my realtor."

"I had planned to, but…" He crossed the room. "Gwen, I'm sorry about before."

"We've done this already…"

"Please just let me finish." He squatted before her and took her hand in his. "When I left for boot camp I thought we'd be together forever. Once things were official and I made it through my training, then we'd get married. It wasn't until I was actually there that I realized you deserved so much better. It wasn't the training, or the long hours, it was what I saw the other guys going through with their families. I knew things would only get worse as my SEAL training continued."

"What are you saying?"

"We didn't talk about it much but I knew you wanted a family of your own. I could have given you that, the house you wanted, all the material things, but what I couldn't give you was me. Training day in and day out for over two years. Since then it's been missions and more training, a SEAL's job is never done. How could I expect you to sit idly by at home and wait for me, never knowing what I was doing or if I'd even survive? That was no life for you."

"Why do we have to do this again?" Tears glistened in her eyes.

"Because you need to understand." He squeezed her hand. "It was the hardest decision I ever made, but one I thought was right for you. The whole family gave me shit about it. Everyone thought I was making a huge mistake, hell even I thought I was. You were always the best thing in my life. I thought I was making the best decision for you."

"You could have talked to me about this, given me some say in the matter. Instead you sent me a letter."

"I wrote the letter because I knew if I didn't do it then I wouldn't be able to. I planned to explain when I was on leave…then I just couldn't come home and face you. By then I knew I made a mistake."

The tears were falling down her face. "We all make mistakes and they can be forgiven. You should have come to me."

"How could I? By doing what I thought was right, I broke your heart. I screwed everything up."

"Someone once told me that you can go back to the place where it all went wrong and find your way again."

He blinked, trying to determine if he'd heard her correctly. Did she mean there was still a chance for them? He was supposed to be making amends with her so he could put the space between them without additional hard feelings. He wasn't supposed to be getting involved with her.

He stayed where he was, the grandfather clock in the entryway ticking the seconds off as if reminding him there wouldn't be another chance. If he screwed up this time, it would be the end of anything he could have with Gwen.

"When I first received the letter I was upset, angry, and heartbroken. Who knows what would have happened between us. I knew about your ambitions to be a SEAL since that first day, and that didn't stop me from falling in love with you." She placed her index finger under his chin and gently guided it up until their gazes met. "So what if you were gone more than you were home, it would just make us cherish the moments we had together that much more. If the love is true and strong, it can overcome anything."

"I thought you deserved someone home with you each night, someone who could be an actual father to your children. To throw a ball with the boys and to scare off any dates the daughters might have."

"As noble as the thought was, it should have been *our* decision to make, not yours. I don't think it worked out as you wanted it to anyway." She smirked and laid her hand on the top curve of her stomach.

"Maybe not how I had hoped, but what matters is your happiness." He laid his hand over hers on her stomach. "I know how important children were for you."

"If you're seeking my forgiveness, you have it. I made peace with what happened a while ago."

"Forgiveness is great in its own way, but that's not the reason I'm telling you this. It should have been done a long time ago. I should have told you so you understood why. It had nothing to do with anything you did...or because I didn't love you."

Even as he sat before her, he realized he'd loved her then and he still loved her. That was what made the situation so much more difficult.

Capturing a Diamond – SEALed for You

Chapter Six

Curled up in front of the fire with a warm blanket, Gwen laid the book on her lap and let her head rest against the back of the sofa. It was a perfect evening, one she had been having almost every night this week. She couldn't resist curling up with a good book in front of the fire, but tonight was different. She couldn't get her thoughts away from Ace.

Even after having her heartbroken by him, she couldn't get him out of her system. She longed to feel his touch. If only they could pick up where they left off. She dragged her hand through her spiky hair and enjoyed the moment. At least the tension that had been there before was gone.

"Why didn't you tell me you bumped into Lucky?"

His words pulled her from her thoughts. "You sidetracked me when I got in and I forgot. He wanted me to pass on the invitation to his place for dinner. You're supposed to text him your response tonight so he knows."

He held up his cell phone. "I know. He just texted me. He suggested I send you to bed without supper, like Mom always threatened, for not telling me."

"Your mom would have never done that."

"No, but she threatened. So, little lady, shall I force you to bed?"

Her hormones were playing with her heart and soul; if she wasn't careful they'd lead her to dangerous waters. "Try me, if you're man enough."

He tossed his phone aside and stalked toward her. "That sounds like a challenge. One I think I should take you up on." Taking hold of her hand, he pulled her up out of the chair, the blanket sliding down her legs to land in a pile at their feet.

"Ace."

"Yes?" He scooped her into his arms.

"Put me down." Instead of doing what she asked, he pretended to drop her, forcing her to squeal. "Ace Le Diamond, I demand you put me down." She tried to fill her voice with authority but it was hard with his cologne filling each breath.

"You know I won't drop you."

"What are you doing?" She resisted the urge to rest her head against his strong chest. "You're not putting me to bed."

"It's been so long and I've missed you. Is it wrong that I just want to feel you against me?" He sank down onto the sofa, taking her with him. "If it is, I don't want to be right. I just want to hold you. Is that too much to ask?"

"No, it's not." She let herself relax in his embrace, her head resting on the curve of his shoulder. She began to wonder what it might have been like if they'd never drifted apart. Maybe they'd be sharing this same moment as a married couple, the child she was expecting his. Fantasies, yes—but it was what she wanted.

His lips brushed against the top of her forehead. "This is nice."

She leaned away and looked into his eyes, hoping to find the answer she needed. She needed to know if she was just another girl to fill the time before he left again, or if there were feelings within him that burned for her.

"I can't do this."

"What?"

"I can't..." She took a deep breath and pushed away the tears. "Ace, I never stopped loving you. All these years I waited for you, hoping one day you'd see reason and come back. When I woke up from the coma, you were the one person I wanted at my bedside, but then I realized it was never going to happen. Instead of giving my heart away to another, I buried it deep within me and decided to do this alone."

She ran her hand over her stomach, knowing she had to do this not only for herself but for her daughter. They couldn't live in the same town together if he broke her heart again. "I can't do this because I can't risk you going off on your next training or mission or whatever the hell you want to call it and deciding what's best for me."

"Wait." With one arm, he held tight as she tried to wiggle out of his embrace. He reached behind him, grabbing his wallet. "Every day I've carried this with me." He pulled out a creamy white ribbon with pink stitches along the edges. "It's my lucky charm, always keeping me safe, no matter how dangerous things get. I never stopped loving you."

Seeing that ribbon sent her memories racing back to that night, only hours before he shipped off to boot camp. They'd sat on the beach, watching the waves crash onto the shore, his arm around her. Back then, it wasn't supposed to be goodbye, only a short time apart until his training was over. Even knowing he was supposed to come back and they'd be together again, her heart broke.

He untied her hair from the ribbon, letting it down to blow in the wind, and whispered sweet promises in her ear. Promising they'd be together forever, he tied the ribbon around his wrist and pushed her gently back onto the blanket, kissing her.

"Do you remember what happened that night?"

His words pulled her back from the memories. It was the first and only time they made love. She lost her virginity to a man she thought she'd spend the rest of her life with. One who ended up leaving without so much of an explanation.

"I remember." As much as it warmed her heart to know he had kept that with him, it didn't change things. "I remember what happened that night, but what is more important is what happened after…"

"Gwen." He slid his hand down her thigh. "I made a mistake, but there's no reason we should suffer from my stupidity any longer. We deserve a second chance."

"Ace." She cupped his cheek, feeling the smooth skin under her fingertips, and gazed into his forest green eyes. "I can't...it's too much for me. I'm sorry, but I can't risk you breaking my heart again when you leave. You said it yourself, you're only home for three days, then you'll leave again and the same thing will happen."

Unable to sit there any longer, she slipped from his embrace, putting distance between them. She needed to be alone, so she grabbed her coat from the hall closet before heading out the front door.

It might not have been the smartest move, but it preserved her heart. Forcing away the tears, she thrust her hands into her pockets and tried to steady her breathing. Following her urges could land her back in the same position she'd been in all those years ago. There was no way she'd let that happen again.

Capturing a Diamond – SEALed for You

Chapter Seven

Ace stood there stunned beyond belief as he watched Gwen storm out of the house. It was unlike her to face a problem head on. Unwilling to screw this up again, he slipped his shoes on and decided to follow her. He understood where she was coming from, but damn he wanted her. Having her body pressed against his made everything come back. His job was dangerous and the commitment she needed was one he wasn't sure he'd be able to give…no matter how much he wanted to. Even so, he had to make it clear how much he cared.

Outside he looked both directions but couldn't see her anywhere. How she had managed to disappear when he was only minutes behind her, he had no idea. Going with his gut he headed to the park, imagining it would give her a place to sit and think. Not wanting to lose her, he took off in a steady jog, scanning each side street as he past.

Three blocks later, he entered a picturesque neighborhood, fall leaves scattered on the ground. It was quiet, deserted at that time of night. Headlights illuminated a few small brick houses, then the small car motored off. Just down the path on one of the benches that overlooked the playground area was Gwen, her hand rubbing small circles over her stomach. The dim light caught the glistening tears running down her face.

Damn it, this is why I left. I never wanted to cause her pain, but here I am screwing up her life again.

He needed to make it right. If she chose not to pursue things between them, he'd have to respect that, but until he said what he needed to, he wouldn't back down. If things were going to work between them, she had to be able to accept everything as it was—his job and their past.

"Gwen…" He sat down on the bench next to her and kept his gaze on the playground before him. She barely acknowledged him. "Years ago, I screwed up. I should have been upfront and discussed things with you. Instead, I made the decision without even consulting you. It was wrong of me, but I thought I was doing what was best for you."

"What's done is done, none of it matters now." Her voice broke.

"It does." He turned and laid a hand over hers. "I don't deserve it, but I believe we were given this second chance for a reason."

"I have a child to think about," she snapped. "I wouldn't just be risking myself but my daughter. I can't…"

"We have months before she's born, let's take time to explore things between us." He laced his fingers through hers. "I can see the look in your eyes. There's still something between us, and it's not just hard feelings. Tell me you don't still love me and I'll let it go."

"I…" She shook her head, then wiped her nose.

"See, I knew you couldn't, because I can't deny it either." He scooted closer to her on the bench, closing that last remaining distance.

"Maybe love isn't enough." She wouldn't look at him as she said it, giving him the impression she didn't believe it.

"Let me prove to you that is it." They sat there in silence for what seemed like ages, but finally he couldn't wait any longer. "I understand it doesn't seem like enough. Maybe what I can give you isn't what you want, but I do love you. Being a SEAL is who I am. If I thought anyone would understand, it would be you."

"I've never asked you to give it up. It's what you've always wanted, and now you have it. Was it worth what you lost?"

"Is it wrong to want everything?" He turned on the bench so that he could look at her. "When I left, you were only seventeen. I had planned to complete my training and come back for you. To marry you and give you everything you ever wanted. I wanted to wait until I knew I could do it, because if I failed…I didn't know what I'd do."

"I knew you wouldn't fail, it's not who you are." For the first time she met his gaze, telling him she had more faith in him than anyone else. "You worked so hard to prepare yourself before you left. I never doubted you."

"I failed in the one part that mattered most. I failed you, Gwen." As the tears streamed down her face, he pulled her against his chest, holding her as if she was all he had left. "No excuse changes that." He let her tears subside before adding, "Let me prove I'm worthy of you. This time I won't make the same mistake."

With her arm around his waist, she kept her head pressed against his chest. "I don't think the timing is right. I'm pregnant." There wasn't regret in her voice but maybe disappointment, as if she thought they'd miss their second chance at love.

"On the contrary, I think it's the perfect time. Give *us* a chance. There's no other way to prove to you that it won't happen again, unless you give us a chance." He ran his hand along the curve of her back, hoping she wouldn't turn away from him.

"You'll leave and things will end again. I can't take that pain." Her voice broke. She pulled back from his embrace, biting hard on her bottom lip. "I don't care what people say. It *isn't* better to have loved and lost."

"There's a reason we were brought back together, that my mission ended early and you were here." He gazed down at her and hated that the tears were because of him. "Let's take it slow. Seventy-two hours isn't enough time for me to convince you, but when I come back from this training, I should be home for a while, unless a mission comes up. Then you'll know I'm not going to make the same mistake and I'll have time to properly show you what you mean to me."

"Slow, okay?" The tears were gone now, faint lines marking her face where they fell.

He nodded and kissed her forehead. "Whatever pace you want is fine with me. Come, let's go home, sit by the fire and warm up. On the way, you can tell me about your home search today. Lucky mentioned you were looking at a condo in his building." He kept his arm around her waist and led her back the way they had come.

"My realtor, Trudy, showed me a few places," she mumbled, her head against his chest. "One of them was the condo next to Lucky's. I thought I wanted a house, but this place had everything I wanted and more. The views are good considering it's not right on the beach, but the roof top deck is amazing. If I want it, I'll have to make an offer soon."

"Lucky says the place is quiet most of the time. I think he's the only bachelor living there. Don't let his bitching about that confuse you, he loves it. Everyone takes such good care of him. I don't think he's ever had to cook a meal. Someone is always bringing him something, checking on his place while he's deployed. He's got it too good there, it's almost like living with Mom, but with more freedom."

"Your mom taught both of you how to cook. Why's he letting others do so much for him?"

"Cooking for one loses its appeal quickly. He repays the favor either with his delicious desserts, or by doing something else for them." He chuckled to himself at the life his little brother was living. Carefree and fun was the best way to describe it.

"I remember those desserts he used to make. If he still has that same sweet tooth, I'm surprised he's in such good shape. I don't think he has an ounce of fat on him."

"It's his training. He might have it easier than me, but he still works off those sweets." He tried to laugh it off, knowing that Lucky was in just as much danger as he was on some missions. He might be deployed less frequently, but the Marines were still the first ones to a battle.

Not wanting to remind her just how dangerous his career was, he teased his fingers along the curve of her shoulder and changed the subject. "Maybe you should hold off putting an offer on a house."

"What?" She tipped her head back to look up at him.

"There's no reason you can't stay here." He kept his fingers moving over her shoulder, hiding his worry that she'd reject the idea. "I can deal with the shit in the guest room and it could be set up as a nursery. More importantly it will keep you close."

"That's too quick." She tensed under his touch. "Plus I have stuff in storage waiting for me to find a place."

"Just hold off until I'm back from this training."

"Why is it so important to you?"

"In my career, time is limited. I want to spend every opportunity I can with you, to show you what you mean to me." When she said nothing, he added, "The training will only be seven days. That's nothing when you're thinking about the purchase of a house."

"Okay. Unless the perfect place comes on the market, I'll hold off putting a bid in."

"Thank you." A ding from the cell phone in his pocket reminded him the guys were probably wondering where he was. He didn't care, he had everything he wanted right here. Tomorrow he'd smooth things over with the guys, but for tonight he was going to enjoy every moment he could with Gwen in his arms.

Keeping his arm around her body, he held her close and tried not to think what the morning would bring for them. Exhaustion ate at every part of him, but that wasn't uncommon for him. Instead of sleeping he wanted the moment to last, as if he was worried tomorrow he'd wake up and it would all be a dream.

Capturing a Diamond – SEALed for You

Chapter Eight

There was a certain comfort to sitting across from her while she worked, as Ace went through the mail that had piled up while he was away. It was as if it was always meant to be this way—he and Gwen, together.

The ringing of the doorbell distracted him. "I'll get it." He rose from the table. *Then I'll kill whoever is ruining my peaceful moment.*

Ready to decapitate whoever was at the door, he pulled it open. Leaning against the porch pillar was Boom. They might have been best friends, but he wasn't completely thrilled to see him. It wasn't just the fact that he had interrupted a quiet day with Gwen. Wherever he went, things had a tendency to erupt. He was the team's demolition expert but when he arrived things had a tendency to explode around him, landmines and everything else that got in his way, and he walked away unharmed every time.

"What happened to you last night?" Boom narrowed his eyes, his big arms crossed over his barrel chest.

Ace stepped onto the porch and closed the door behind him; the last thing he wanted was Boom exploding the already delicate situation with Gwen. "I stayed in, not that you were going to be there anyway. Why are you up before sunset?"

"The guys called, seems Rebel got himself into it with a drunk in the parking lot. Our little medic almost ended up in jail."

"Why can't they go out and not cause any problems?" Ace mumbled.

"You remember what it was like."

"Yeah, I remember, but we got the shit kicked out of us for it." He didn't want to think about all the times they had to put in an extra training session because they blew off a little too much steam for their commanding officer to overlook. "Does Mac know?"

"Oh, yeah. He'll ride Rebel hard when we head off for our refresher."

Refresher? What a nice way of putting this shitty training mission. The higher ups ordered Mac and the other COs to conduct an advanced close quarter combat training, after one of the other SEAL teams got jammed up.

"Ace?" He turned to see Gwen peeking out the door. He hadn't even heard it open. "Wynn's on the phone for you."

"Could you tell her I'll call her back?"

"So that's why you didn't go out last night." Boom smirked when Gwen closed the door. "Who's she?"

"Gwen… Gwyneth London. You remember her from school?"

"No way…" Boom stepped closer to the window, trying to peer in. "She looks so different…and pregnant. What she doing here?"

"It's a long story, but she's going to be staying here for a bit." Ace didn't want to get into all the details with Boom, especially since he didn't know where he stood with Gwen.

"Oh man." Boom returned to his spot against the pillar. "Please tell me you aren't getting involved with her."

"What's that supposed to mean?"

"Dude, she's pregnant." Boom stated it as if that made some kind of difference.

"I can see that. How do you know it's not my child?" The words escaped Ace's lips before he had time to think about it, and he realized he wished it was true.

"You mean besides the fact we've been gone over six months? You couldn't hold something like this from me. We've been best friends since third grade. I know you, and you don't need to get involved with an instant family. Man, you don't have to go around saving everyone. Think of yourself for a minute and not about the damsel in distress. Have you stopped to think that maybe she came to you because she knew you'd help her?"

"Boom…" Ace took a deep breath and kept his hands to himself instead of wrapping them around his friend's neck. "We've been friends for a long time, which is why I'm going to let you leave now without killing you."

"You're not thinking…"

"No man, *you're* not thinking. You know nothing about the situation." Ace gritted his teeth, angry that his friend thought so little of Gwen.

"Then tell me. Tell me I'm wrong, and I won't say another word."

"You're wrong. Her mother passed away while we were deployed and she's moving back into town. Wynn told her she could stay here while she was house searching since it was empty. Now I've got to call Wynn, and get ready for a family obligation."

Boom pushed off the pillar and strolled down the steps before turning back to Ace. "If you think that's all there is to it, you're fooling yourself. I saw how she looked at you. There's love in her eyes…stronger than when we were teenagers. Don't think you'll be able to walk away from her like you did before. This time there'll be a child involved and you're too kindhearted for that."

"I'm not walking away this time." Ace growled, his voice edged with anger.

"That proves my point. You think you can save her."

Ace shook his head. "It's not about saving anyone. I love her."

"What about your career? You said before it wasn't fair to her. You couldn't have her and the SEALs. Are you willing to give up being a SEAL?"

"I made a mistake before, there's no reason I can't have both. She never asked me to choose. That was my mistake, one I plan to make up for now."

"A family deserves more than we can give them." With that, Boom turned on his heels and walked back to his truck.

Ace stood there for a long moment wondering if Boom had a point. Then he shook his head and opened the door. It didn't matter what branch of the military, everyone deserved a chance at happiness and a family, and he wasn't about to miss his opportunity. If he was sure of only one thing, it was that he wouldn't get a second chance. There was only now.

Capturing a Diamond – SEALed for You

Chapter Nine

The seventy-two hours that Ace had on leave flew by in the blink of an eye for Gwen. She'd had all this time with him before he left and now they were down to the last hours. She leaned against the dresser while he added the last remaining items to his duffle bag.

"I can feel you drilling holes into my back." He closed up the bag and turned to her. "It's going to be different this time, I swear. Seven days will go quick and I'll be back here holding you tight. Wynn and Lucky are just a phone call away if you need anything."

"I'll be fine. I've been taking care of myself for years." She forced herself to smile and not think of the last time they were in this predicament.

"I'd never doubt it for a moment. I just want you to know you're not alone." He came to her, slipping his arm around her waist.

"Do you need a ride? Maybe I can make you something to eat before you go?"

"Shh, love." He ran the knuckle of his index finger down her cheek and over her chin. "I'll drive myself and leave my truck on base."

"Food?" She wanted something to do, anything to relieve the unease within her.

"Let's go for a walk."

"Shouldn't you…be leaving?"

"I have time." He slipped his hand into hers. "Come with me, there's a place I want to show you."

"Where are we going?" She let him lead her down the steps and through the house. It wasn't until they were out the back door that she paused. It was the first time she had been out back and nothing had changed. The flagstone patio dominated the back of the house, leading to the pool and hot tub on one side, while the other side was set up for outdoor entertaining. Ace's father designed a perfect outdoor kitchen that fit both his and his wife's needs, allowing for a large grill and plenty of space. Off to the side a flagstone path led down to the creek that backed the property. It was the place where they'd first met.

She balked. "Ace…"

"Every deployment I've gone on, there's one thing I always do before I leave. Do you remember why I go down by the creek?" When she didn't answer, he spoke it aloud as if she had forgotten. "It's where we first met. Your friend Madison lived in the house on the other side of the creek. Wynn, Lucky, and I were down there playing…"

"I remember." She nodded. "It was just after I moved here."

"You, Madison, and Wynn were inseparable after that day." He brought her hand to his lips and placed a gentle kiss on her knuckles. "I've never been able to get you off my mind since."

"It's also where we spent many afternoons before you left." The memories poured forth, bringing back all the good times she had with the whole Diamond family.

"It's the place of many firsts for us. The first time we met, our first kiss, the first time I told you I loved you."

"I don't think we should…" She paused and glanced toward the path again. "It could ruin a spot that means a lot to both of us."

"It won't. I told you I'm coming back to you, not even a herd of wild elephants could keep me away from you. Having you join me on the walk will add another first."

"What do you mean?" She raised an eyebrow in question.

"It will be the first time you've seen me off on military duty. Another first for us and one of many I hope."

She nodded. If she was going to trust things would be different this time, she had to make them different. Ace might have been the one to end things, but he wasn't the only one to blame. She could have tried harder to get in touch with him, to convince him they could make things work. Growing up in a military family, she knew firsthand that military life was tough, and there was no doubt in her mind that SEAL life was harder, but Ace was worth it.

Ace leaned against one of the command vehicles while they waited for Lieutenant Mac García to finish dressing down one of the newest team members, Petty Officer Cannon Bailey. From the look of Cannon when he arrived, he'd been out late partying and overslept. The Lieutenant was already going to ride them hard during the training for the scene at the bar the other night, and Cannon's lateness was going to make things worse. Even knowing the next week might resemble *hell week* all over again, Ace didn't care…he could only think about getting back to Gwen.

Damn, that woman had him all turned around with need and desire. Fantasies of getting her naked haunted him day and night. The only thing that had kept it from happening was promising they'd take things slow. After this mission, she'd trust him more and he could get her into his bed.

"How's your instant family?" Boom leaned against the vehicle, watching the other men load the final things onto the plane.

"Don't call Gwen that." Ace glared at Boom and tried to keep from hitting his best friend.

"Man, you left her for a reason. Why are you setting both of you up to get hurt? She deserves better than that."

"I was young and stupid." He was still upset after the last time they had this conversation and didn't want to get into it again with Boom. "I'm not going to screw this up."

"I hope you know what you're doing."

"Just drop it, Boom, this has *nothing* to do with you." Ace's anger was starting to seep into his voice. He was tired of Boom's attitude, and he was sick of the instant family comment. The only thing that stopped him from saying more was García strolling toward them.

Time to get this going…

Capturing a Diamond – SEALed for You

Chapter Ten

With a deep sigh, Gwen tossed her purse and keys on the table.

The first appointment with her new OBGYN had gone well. Her baby girl was healthy and developing right on schedule. In less than five months, she'd have a child to make a life for. So it was now or never for her and Ace to work things out. If he screwed up this time, that was it.

With her feet killing her, she strolled around the living room to the sofa and plopped down. Kicking off her heels, she leaned back against the soft throw pillows and longed for a nap. The flashing of the answering machine caught her attention.

Maybe it's Ace. She leaned forward and pressed the glowing red light. Instantly, Ace's voice filled the room.

"I've only got a minute but I remembered you mentioning your appointment was today. Hope everything went great and you can tell me about it soon." Something in the background of the call made

Ace pause before continuing. "Don't wait up. It will be late tomorrow when I get back. I miss you."

Just that brief message served to lighten her heart, knowing he was safe. It made her long for him to be with her, to have him share in the moment of her pregnancy, even though it wasn't his child. Finally, she understood how her mother felt anytime there was word from her father, even if it was only a message or a letter. Her dad had missed so many important moments in her life, including most of her parents' anniversaries, and still their family stayed strong, even though the times were tough. Her mom always said military families were made stronger, or else they wouldn't get through it.

The front door creaked open behind her. With no doubt in her mind who it was, she didn't bother to turn around.

"Gwen, you back?" Wynn called out, stepping into the foyer.

"In here."

Wynn sauntered in as if she was hot off a catwalk, always so put together and ready to take on the world. Owning a fashionable boutique—Roll of the Diamond—just off the boardwalk, she had to flaunt her designs. It was perfect for Wynn because she wouldn't be caught dead in jeans and a T-shirt.

How the two of them became inseparable was beyond Gwen. They couldn't have been more different. Where Wynn was a girly girl, Gwen was slightly tomboyish, and preferred her jeans rather than slacks or dresses.

"I brought Pete's Pizza." Wynn sat the box down on the coffee table, and pulled two bottles of water from a bag. "Have you heard from Ace?"

"Today, he'll be home tomorrow late night." Gwen leaned forward and opened the pizza box, revealing the delicious square slices. The squares were thick like pan pizza but crispy and light, and each one could have its own toppings. It was her favorite pizza place and one she'd missed when she moved away.

"Normally he's not able to call much, so it's nice he was able to this time," Wynn said.

"He called the day he left too." She grabbed a slice before leaning back against the sofa, and took a bite. "I know it's not always like this, and there will be times he's gone for a lot longer where I won't hear from him, but it was nice he called."

"I only mentioned it because I want you to understand what you are getting yourself and your daughter into. Is Ace really the man you want?"

"Oh, Wynn." Suddenly disgusted by the pizza, she tossed it back into the box.

"Think of me as a friend, not as Ace's sister. Don't get me wrong, it would be amazing to have things work out for you two and to have you as a sister-in-law, but I just want you to know what you're doing. I remember how distraught you were when he cut ties between you two. I don't want to see you go through that again."

"I never stopped loving him. All this time there's never been anyone else, only him."

"You mean…"

"No one." She nodded. "I've dated occasionally but there's never been anyone else I've been intimate with. Why do you think I chose to have a sperm donor? I had no other choice. Other men didn't compare to Ace. They did nothing for me. My heart and body belonged to him."

"You grew up in a military family, are you sure you want that for your daughter?" Wynn perched on the edge of the recliner.

"You didn't grow up with it being engraved into your life like I did. Dad only retired because his health started to decline, otherwise he'd have stayed in until he died. It was his life." She ran her hand over her stomach. "Dad was away a lot and even when he was home he worked crazy hours, but that didn't change how I felt about him. When he was there, he spoiled mom and me, and every moment with him was even more special and cherished."

"You didn't answer me, is that what you want for your daughter?" Wynn pushed.

"I want a life where we're happy. My daughter should grow up surrounded by family and love, where she can become whatever she wants. I'm going to take things one step at a time with Ace, and we'll go from there. If things work out, wonderful…if not, my daughter will have me and I'll have to be enough." She cracked open one of the bottles of water and took a sip. "Ace doing his duty for the country, keeping each of us safe, is an amazing thing. It wouldn't diminish his role in our lives but would make it stronger. We would cherish the time we have with him. He's a hero."

Wynn smirked. "Don't take me asking as I'm trying to keep the two of you apart. You're my best friend, and like a sister to me, I don't want to see you get hurt again. The last time it caused a riff in the relationship between Ace and me, and we're just getting back to where we were. I don't think it can take another hit like the last time, and I don't want to have to beat the shit out of him again."

"What?"

"Mom and I went to see him for a weekend, it was a couple weeks after you received the letter."

"Tell me you didn't."

Wynn nodded. "I confronted him. Words weren't enough, but when it turned to a fight, it was only my fists flying. He ended up with a black eye and busted lip. It would have been worse but Mom stopped it."

"You shouldn't have done it."

"Why?" Wynn leaned forward, putting her elbows on her knees. "He did wrong by you. A damn letter? Seriously? Mom taught all of us better than that. You should have heard the lecture Dad gave him."

"I never wanted to cause problems in the family." She hated the idea that his family said something to him about what happened. It should have stayed between them, but since she confided in Wynn, it got back to the whole Diamond family. "He did what he thought was best."

"Don't defend his actions, he broke your heart."

"What's more important is he's mending my heart now." Gwen ran her hand down the bottle, wiping away the moisture. She didn't want to think about the past. Right now was a time for new beginnings. In order to do that she had to give up the ghosts of the past.

"What if he breaks it again?"

"Then that's it. I'll pick up the pieces and move on for the sake of my daughter." She set the bottle aside and met Wynn's gaze. "Could we please drop this? The past is what it is. Nothing can change that, but this is a second chance for Ace and me. Couldn't you just be happy for us?"

"I want to be, but I keep thinking about that damn letter."

"I appreciate your concern, but I want to give this a try. I love Ace." As soon as the words left her mouth, she knew it was true. The love for him never ceased or diminished. She loved him and wanted this to work out. They'd make it work.

Chapter Eleven

It was just after two in the morning when Ace pulled into the driveway of his house. Only the light above the door glowed bright through the dark night, welcoming him. For the first time in his career, there was someone waiting for him to come home. Never before did the idea of having someone there appeal to him.

He opened the truck door, thinking of slipping into bed next to Gwen. The notion of feeling her warm body pressed against his hardened his shaft with desire. He reached across the seat and tugged his duffle bag out with him. When he turned around, the front door opened and Gwen stood in the doorway wearing gray yoga pants, a skimpy tank top, and a blanket around her shoulders.

"You didn't have to wait up." Seeing her sent a rush of energy through him. There was a lightness to his steps as he came up the pathway to the house.

"I was in bed when I saw your lights." She stepped out of the way, giving him space to enter. There was an uneasy smile etched on her face, almost like she wasn't sure how to handle the homecoming.

Wanting to ease the tension quickly, he tossed his bag on the floor, kicked the door shut, and went to her. Wrapping his arms around her, he pulled her tight against him. "I've missed you." He almost told her he loved her, but the last thing he wanted was for her to run out the door scared.

"You mean you were gone?" She teased, clinging to him. She ran her hands up his back, as if she was trying to convince herself he was there.

"I know that look in your eye. You missed me." He kissed the top of her head. "Come sit for a moment and tell me how your appointment went. Did you find a house this past week? How much did you miss my arms around you?" He spouted off the questions before she could answer them.

She pulled the blanket tighter around her shoulders and moved to the sofa. "Everything is fine with my pregnancy. My daughter is healthy and growing right on schedule. Though this made me realize I need to figure out a name for her. Other than the appointment, the week was rather quiet. I did see two other places, but the condo next to Lucky's is still my first choice."

"Why not stay here?" He pulled her into his lap and linked his arms around her waist. "I told you this time would be different. Stay with me."

She leaned her head against his shoulder and let out a soft laugh. "My parents would roll over in their graves if they knew I was shacking up with a man before marriage."

"Then marry me."

Her head popped up and her eyes widened. "What?"

"Hear me out." He held tight as she started to pull away from him. "I've done a lot of thinking this past week. If I wouldn't have screwed up, you'd be my wife, and this would be our child."

"But that's not the case." Sorrow coated her words.

"Not yet, but there's no reason it can't be. You deserve so much better, but I realized this is all I can give you. If you allow me, I'll spend the rest of my life proving you didn't make a mistake. Gwen, I love you. You've always had my heart."

Tears glistened in her eyes. "I love you too."

"Then marry me."

"There's more to marriage than just love. I'm pregnant with another man's child."

He placed his hand on the curve of her stomach, feeling the roundness under his fingers. "Let me be a father to her."

"I thought we were taking this slow." She smirked. "This isn't slow."

"Then just think about it. When you're ready, the offer stands. If we marry before you give birth, she can have the Diamond name and no one needs to know otherwise. She'll be my daughter in every way."

"I need to think about this." She laid her hand over his. "I'm not ashamed of using a sperm donor…"

"Gwen, that's not what I meant. I only meant that if you let me, she would be my daughter in every way. She's a part of you, and I'll love her just like I love you." It didn't matter the child wouldn't be his flesh and blood; she would still be his daughter.

"What about your family?"

He raised an eyebrow in confusion. Wynn and Lucky already knew she was pregnant and it wasn't his, but neither of them had said anything about it. He wasn't sure where her worry was coming from.

"What about them?"

"Wynn stopped by yesterday. She mentioned the two of you got into it pretty good a few weeks after I received the letter."

"I remember. I ended up with a black eye. Even Lucky took a few hits when I saw him. But what does that have to do with right now?"

"Your father laid into you about it too."

He nodded. "I'm still missing the connection."

"I caused all these problems because I shared what happened with Wynn. I never expected her to tell everyone. Oh, your family must hate me."

"It was never your fault, only mine. They don't hate you." He wiped the tears from her cheeks. "During that visit where Wynn took her anger out on my face, Mom told me she always expected we'd get married. She wasn't happy with how I went about things, but she believed things would work out in the end. Maybe if I would have come home sooner, it would have worked out long before now."

"What matters is now."

"Then let's just enjoy that I'm home and you're by my side."

"What did you have in mind?" Her glossy pink lips curled up into a smile.

"Let me take you to bed. I want to hold you close while we sleep. Then in the morning, let's just see what happens then."

"Hmm, morning." She winked at him before slipping off his lap to stand. "I'm tired, so if you're coming..."

"Oh sugar, I'm coming." He took hold of her hand. "I wouldn't miss this for the world."

He didn't care if it took his whole life, he'd convince her he was there for the long haul. Their past was rocky and there were things they'd have to overcome, but they could do it together. The love he had for her was strong enough they could overcome anything. This was the life he was supposed to have years ago and now he was claiming it. He wasn't going to let Gwen slip through his fingers again.

Capturing a Diamond – SEALed for You

Chapter Twelve

Dressed in a little black cocktail dress that hid the slight curve of Gwen's growing stomach, she fingered the strand of her mother's pearls around her neck, feeling sexier than ever. She checked the mirror again to make sure her hair was spiking in all the right places, before slipping into the heels she had set out. She wanted everything perfect. Going to Wynn's for a small gathering seemed to add more pressure to her relationship with Ace.

Wynn was her best friend, but this one time Gwen wished she'd lay off. She needed time with Ace to work things out. Not to mention time to think about the marriage proposal.

"Gwen?" Ace called from the downstairs landing. "Are you ready yet?"

"Men are always so impatient," she told her daughter, running her hand over her stomach. With one final check, she turned and headed downstairs.

Exiting her room, she found Ace at the top of the stairs. "I heard that."

"You must have hearing like a dog, I barely said it aloud." He stood there with his mouth open, staring at her like he'd never seen her before. "Why are you looking at me like that?"

"Wow." He opened and closed his mouth. "You look beautiful."

"You act like this is the first time ever." Nervous, she bit her lip, waiting for him to stop looking at her like a freak event at a zoo.

"Not the first time, but damn, woman, you blow me away." He closed the distance between them and slipped his arms around her waist. "What do you say about staying in tonight and letting me take you back to bed?"

As tantalizing as that offer sounded, she shook her head. "Tempting, but we made a promise that we'd be at Wynn's tonight."

"Someday my workaholic sister will understand." He leaned his head down into the crest of her shoulder, his warm breath against her skin sending a line of goosebumps down her arm. "Wouldn't you rather stay in and let me cherish your body, make love to you until you scream my name?"

"You've been home two days and now you want me?" She tried to sound hurt but it wasn't working. Every word held a hind of desire rather than disappointment.

"Sweets, I've wanted you, but you wanted to take this slow. It's been incredibly hard but I wanted to do right by you." He kissed her neck, gently dragging his teeth over her skin. "I want you now."

She curled her neck into him, drawing his mouth closer, and a soft moan escaped her lips. Need and desire coursed through her, until she was almost willing to forget the dinner and let him take her. "Ace…"

"Yes?" He kissed along her neck until he reached her earlobe.

"Tonight. After Wynn's. Let's go before my control snaps."

"That's almost an invitation to keep going. Once your control is gone we can forget going out and make it up to Wynn later." He stepped back, and straightened his dress shirt. "Let's get this over with."

"You should be happy to spend the evening with your family."

"She's inviting us to see how things are progressing with us. Wynn has always been the nosiest of all of the Diamond clan." He slipped his hand in hers, and headed for the steps.

"You do realize that is a *major* accomplishment, right?"

He stopped halfway down the steps and raised an eyebrow at her. "Are you saying my family is a bunch of nosy busybodies?"

"Oh, look at the time, we need to be going." She slipped past him, quickly coming down the last steps.

"Gwyneth London." There was a playfulness in his tone as he called after her. "Don't you walk away from me."

"On the risk of repeating myself, we need to be going."

"Answer me, then we can go." He came down the final steps.

"You're not blind, you know what your family is like better than me." She opened the closet door and grabbed their coats. "Lucky and you aren't much better than Wynn."

He took her coat and held out it for her. "I'm going to make you pay for that comment tonight."

"Promises, promises." She handed him his coat and waited while he buttoned the double breast jacket.

It was amazing they were able to have such ease between them after what had separated them. If only the ease would continue through the rest of the family. She hadn't told Ace about the conversations she had with Lucky and Wynn urging her to stay away from him, because she didn't want to cause any problems between the siblings. Things were going so well now, she could only hope they held their tongues tonight, and didn't bring up what happened when he went off to boot camp.

Ace stood on the balcony, the salty breeze from the ocean beating against him, cooling the desires that ran through him. His last shred of control was hanging by a thin thread, and every ounce of him wanted to rush back inside and whisk Gwen away. In his line of work he could be called into action any time, and all he could think about was having Gwen naked beneath him before he had to leave again.

The way that short black dress hugged every curve of her body had his shaft hard since she'd stepped out of the bedroom. He never wanted something as much as he wanted her that very moment. Damn Wynn for inviting them. Keeping him here was pure torture.

"We need to talk." Lucky closed the balcony door behind him.

"Then talk." It came out edgier than he meant, but he didn't want to talk, especially not about what Lucky thought they needed privacy for.

"Man, I think you're wrong. Gwen doesn't need this. She doesn't need to have her heart broken again. You weren't around to see what it did to her before, but I was. You either stay with her, or leave her alone. Don't screw with her, she deserves better than that."

"This isn't your business. Stay out of it, Lucky." He clenched the wrought iron banister, refusing to give into his brother's taunts.

"You weren't here before. I was. That makes it my business. Wynn and I helped her put the pieces together. She was a mess, and I don't want to see her go through that again."

Ace spun toward his brother and let the anger flow through him. If Lucky wasn't going to back off, Ace had to make him do it out of self-preservation. "If I didn't know any better I'd think you had something for her. All those years when she was alone you didn't make your move, but now I'm back and you're jealous. I'll kick your ass if I need to, but this is between Gwen and me."

"You fuck this up and it's going to be about all of us. I won't stand by if I think you're hurting her. Wynn and Dad have my back on this, don't think you'll get off like you did before." Lucky turned back to the door, and grabbed hold of the handle. "Don't mess this up."

"What about Mom?"

"What about her?" Lucky glanced back in question.

"You said Wynn and Dad, but you didn't mention Mom. I heard it all from her before, but you left her out of it."

"Mom is the optimistic one of the family, she thinks this is going to work out and you'll be the first of the Diamond crew to get married." Lucky made it obvious he didn't agree, then opened the door and went back inside, leaving Ace alone on the balcony to consider things.

Married? If only I can convince Gwen...

Chapter Thirteen

Ace was still standing on the balcony, his fingers tight around the banister as he stared off at the endless ocean. The sun had set long ago, only leaving darkness in its wake, but with the lights from the condominiums, it was still bright enough to see the waves crash on the beach. The beach was the only appealing thing about Wynn's condo, but he couldn't give up the family home to move and be surrounded by people. When he was home and the SEAL team wasn't there, he needed the quiet; it helped him center himself.

He closed his eyes, taking in the thundering rush of the waves and the draw of the ocean. The sea could be deadly if someone forgot that even for an instant. Reminding him of his job. Would he only end up leaving Gwen as a widow, grieving for him again? Was it fair to her? He cursed himself for letting the doubt creep in again.

"You've been out here a while, is everything okay?"

He opened his eyes to find Gwen standing beside him. "I didn't hear you come out."

She slipped her arm around his waist. "Your forehead is all crinkled together in worry, what's wrong?"

"Nothing." He brought her closer to him and wrapped his arms around her. "How late do we have to stay?"

"You'd think after your last deployment you'd want to spend time with them."

"It's you I want to spend time with." He slid his hand down her hip. "Naked time."

"Then let's go."

"Oh, baby." He lowered his head, letting his lips brush softly against hers. "I'm going to make you a very happy woman tonight."

"Are you always so confident?" She teased.

"I'm a SEAL. I've been through *hell week* and survived, so yeah I'm confident. Tonight you'll see I'm not just cocky, but I have what it takes to back it."

With a smirk and a twinkle in her eyes, she stepped back. "Let me say my goodbyes to Wynn and Lucky, and then we can put you to the test."

"You've got five minutes then I'll carry you out of here if I have to." His body responded as she turned to go back into the house.

Oh yeah, baby, it's time to take all doubt out of her mind.

During the drive across town, Gwen couldn't shake the anger over Wynn's final words. She'd had it with people telling her how to live, thinking they knew best. This was between her and Ace and they'd find their way through all of it if it was meant to be. Otherwise, she'd have to give up on the fantasy of them together and move on with her life. This was their final shot.

All or nothing, Gwen. Give it everything.

"Are you planning to sit here in the car all night? If so I'm sure we could make this work, though I think a bed might be more comfortable."

Ace's voice pulled her from her thoughts, making her realize they had pulled into the driveway. "Sorry." She grabbed the handle and pulled it open.

He laid his hand on her arm before she could slip out of the car. "Second thoughts?"

"No…not at all. I was just thinking about something else, that's all. Now can we go inside? It's chilly." She got out of the car and shut the door before he could say anything else.

Following her lead, he stepped out of the car and met her by the walkway. "Wynn said something to you, didn't she?" When she didn't reply, he added, "I wish they'd just let us live our lives. I hate that she put doubt in your mind."

Anger and sadness crossed his face, pulling at her heart until she reached out and cupped his cheek. "I'm not doubting you."

"I'm going to prove to you…"

"Shh…" She ran her thumb along the line of his jaw, the smooth skin sliding under her fingers like silk. "You've already proven everything to me. Well, except the reason you're so confident."

In answer, he reached down, slid his arm under her legs, and lifted her into his arms. "Let's get this show on the road then."

"Wow, you know I can walk."

"You're a romantic. Don't you want someone to carry you across the threshold?"

She tipped her head back and let out a lighthearted laugh. "That's after a wedding."

"If you'd marry me I'd carry you over every threshold. For now, this will have to do." He winked at her before strolling toward the house, carrying her with ease.

"We'll talk about it after I see how this confidence of yours plays out." She teased him with a wiggle of her eyebrows.

"So my sexual aptitude will decide our marriage." Still holding her, he managed to unlock the door and step inside. "SEALs have stamina unknown to others. I'll have you screaming my name all night."

"Promises, promises." She teased. Their night together before he shipped off for training was special, but something about the way he acted made her think this was going to blow her world.

He kicked the door shut and swung the lock home. "In a moment, it will be more than just words."

"Let me down."

"Not until you're upstairs and laid out on the bed ready for me." Dashing up the steps two at a time, she used her free hand to work on the buttons of his dress shirt. "Then I'll have my way with you."

In the bedroom, he gently placed her on the bed and in one quick move pulled her dress over her head. "Lay back."

"Are you always so demanding?"

"Comes with the territory." He stood there waiting for her to do as he asked, giving her one final chance to back out.

She kicked off her shoes and moved back to the middle of the bed, then leaned back on her elbows waiting for him to join her. "If we're going to be demanding, then you should be just as naked as I am. Out of the dress shirt and jeans."

He tugged the shirt apart, sending the remaining buttons flying. "Is that what you had in mind, sweets?" He unhooked his jeans and let them slid down his hips and onto the floor, until he was standing there in just his boxers with his shaft stretching against the material.

With a shake of her head, she tried to hold back the laughs. "Not entirely, but it works. Now come here."

Without delay, he flopped onto the bed and slid on top of her. "Are you sure about this?"

"Second thoughts?" She started to move up the bed, away from him, and swallowed the fears that were rising within her.

"Not about you, sweets." He pressed his lips to her forehead, sending heat racing through her body.

Laying her hand against his chest, she played with the little patch of hair in the center of his pecs. "I never thought we'd be here…us after all these years, who'd have thought?"

"All that matters is that we are." He reached between her breasts and unhooked her bra. "Now lay back and let me prove I'm worthy to be your husband. Remember that marriage proposal depends on my performance."

She pulled another pillow from the side and shoved it under her head. "I'm waiting."

Their lips met in a long, slow, deliberate kiss that gave and demanded. He cupped her breasts and teased the nipples, gently swirling his thumbs against the hard buds and then pinching them. Pain mingled with pleasure and her back arched. She forgot about the pressures everyone was putting on them and just enjoyed the moment, feeling what Ace was offering her.

His warm laughter washed over her and he abandoned her mouth, sucking one nipple against his teeth. Sparks of pleasure fired inside of her. She hadn't felt anything like this since that night on the beach. Everything inside of her wanted to speed his touch, while another part wanted to enjoy every second as if it could be her last.

He slid his hand under the thin material of her panties and between her thighs, urging them apart. Until his fingers could slide between her folds, finding her special spot, he teased the hard bundle of nerves. His mouth work on one nipple, kissing along the valley between before making his way to the other, all the while his fingers worked to wrench an orgasm from her.

"Ohhh…"She cried out at the climax. The air sizzled around her as he drove her toward the brink again. Opening her eyes, her pleasure soaked gaze found him straddled above her, smirking.

Capturing a Diamond – SEALed for You

Chapter Fourteen

Gwen threw caution to the wind and slipped her hand down his

chest until she could take his shaft in her hand. Wrapping her fingers

around him, she slowly slid her hand over his length. With every

touch, she embraced the life she wanted. This time she wouldn't give

up Ace without a fight.

Her body craved his touch and it had been too long since she

felt the gentle caress of another. He pulled his mouth from hers and

kissed a path down her neck. Sensations collided and threatened to

overwhelm her when he teased her nipples. He slipped on top of her,

breaking her hold on him. His bulky frame hovered above her and he

stared down at her, desire burning in his eyes.

He caressed every inch of her body, sending moans of ecstasy

from her lips. For such a big man, he was incredibly tender, as

though trying to memorize every curve of her body with his hands and mouth. Heat soared through her blood and she grew impatient with need, demanding.

"Ace, I want you."

"Not yet." He slipped down her body until he was at her waist. "Soon, first I want to make this memorable. The first of many..."

He blazed a hot, wet trail of kisses across her belly and stroked her thighs with his fingertips. With every touch, she arched her hips, demanding more. She couldn't get enough of him. Nudging her legs farther apart, he cupped her core. His fingers delved inside her and she met the teasing thrusts. A demanding moan she barely recognized vibrated in her throat. Passion drove fire through her, melting the chill in her center. The trail of wicked kisses tingled over her thighs. He moved his hand and replaced it with his mouth. Tiny nips and gentle licks flicked over her sweet spot, nearly driving her over the edge. She grabbed the top of his head, torn between pressing him closer and dragging him up. She wanted all of him.

"Ace, please..." Even in the sexual haze, she realized what she said and those few words changed everything. There was no going back from sex, but in that moment she didn't care, she wanted him inside her.

"All right, sweets." He spread her legs farther before filling her slowly, inch by inch. Halfway in, he slid out before thrusting, filling her completely with his manhood. His strokes fed her fire like tinder set to dynamite.

His hips increased pace, driving the force of each pump. The thrusts became deeper and faster, falling into a perfect rhythm, moving with such precision, as if in a well-choreographed dance. Their bodies rocked back and forth, tension stretching her tighter as she fought for the release she longed for. She dug her nails into his back, arching her body into his when she came. His rhythm stayed strong until he shouted her name as his own climax followed.

He stayed buried deep within her and leaned down to kiss her forehead. "How was that for a performance?"

"Hmm, I think it could be improved." She teased as he slipped out of her and collapsed beside her.

"I'll see if I can improve next round."

"Not just confident, you jump to assumptions." He slipped his arm around her and pulled her close.

Cuddling tight against Ace, her breath slowly returned to normal, while his fingers caressed her hip in long, lazy strokes. For the first time in a long time, she felt complete. In Ace's arms, she knew she was safe.

"What about the marriage proposal? Did I prove I was worthy of you?"

"You've always been worthy of me." She laid her hand on his chest, teasing along the lines of his abs.

"That doesn't answer my question."

"Ask me properly and you might get an honest answer." She knew the answer she wanted to give, but she wanted it done right.

He smirked at her before pulling his arm from under her head and rolling over. She pulled the sheet over her, hiding her nakedness. "Ace…" Her heart raced. *He couldn't…*

Rolling back over, he held an open ring box. "Gwyneth London, you've had my heart since I found you frolicking down by the creek. Will you do me the honor of marrying me?"

She leaned forward, forgetting the sheet as it slid down her chest, and giving him her left hand. "Yes."

He slipped a beautiful white gold ring onto her finger, with a large princess diamond in the center, surrounded by smaller diamonds. It was completely stunning.

"Before I left for boot camp I bought this."

"Why?" Tears threatened to fall as she gazed down at the ring. After all these years, it was finally happening. She was going to get her prince charming, or maybe that was supposed to be prince SEAL.

"I thought I'd propose before I left."

"Why didn't you?"

"I went to your father and asked his permission." He propped himself up on his elbow, his fingers laced through hers. "He gave it to me, on the condition that I waited until I returned on my first leave."

"Why?" She felt like she was asking the same thing over and over.

"Your parents' marriage was strong but at the beginning it was rough. Your mother didn't understand what she was getting into when she married a military man."

"But I grew up with it, I knew what I was getting into."

"He just wanted to make sure you understood. SEAL life is harder. I could be called up at any time and have to leave on a deployment. He thought the break while I was training would allow you to realize it completely, therefore giving us a solid foot in our marriage. The first year of marriage is always the hardest, especially for military families. He was trying to do right by his only daughter."

"Then he was the first of the crumbling blocks that ended things with us."

"No." He squeezed her hand. "That was completely my fault."

She leaned back against the pillows and drew the back of her hand down his jawline. "Things worked out in the end."

"That they did." He took his hand from hers and laid it on her stomach. "I'd like to marry before…"

"Why is that important?"

"I want this to be prefect. I want *our* daughter to have the Diamond name."

Our daughter.

Her heart skipped a beat. When he'd arrived a few weeks ago, all she could think to do was run, run before he had a chance to break her heart again. Now there she was in bed with him, accepting his proposal, and talking about their daughter. It was almost more than she could believe. Things were nearly perfect. If only Wynn and Lucky could see what was between them without remembering the past.

Capturing a Diamond – SEALed for You

Chapter Fifteen

A roaring fire spread heat through the living room, keeping Gwen cozy as she dozed on the sofa while waiting for Ace to return from the base. Three weeks had passed since she had accepted his proposal, yet they were still keeping it from the rest of the Diamond gang. Wynn's reaction when she found out was going to be the worst of any of them. It was destined to be a disaster.

"Your Auntie Wynn will come around, don't you worry." She rubbed her stomach, trying to calm her daughter. The somersaults were beginning to make her queasy.

Wynn was stubborn and getting her to come around could take time. Lucky would be supportive, but cautious; he was already like a brother to her. The Diamond parents were another story, the unknown factor in the equation. "It's going to be okay." She whispered to herself, trying to calm her nerves.

The front door opened, sending a rush of cold air through the house. "Sweets, I'm home."

"In here." She scooted up on the sofa and tucked her legs under her. "How was work?"

"Same old, same old. Mom called, they're an hour away and very excited to see you again." He'd barely sat in the chair cattycorner from the sofa when he shot up and came to her. "Sweets, are you okay?"

She swallowed the lump in her throat but couldn't quite calm herself.

"You've turned green. You're not worried about Mom?"

"Me, worried?" She tried to make light of it, but her stomach churned.

"Everything is going to be fine. Mom always said we would work things out, and now we have." He cupped her hands. "She's going to be excited this happened, and she's going to be a Grandmother. Anyway, it doesn't matter what anyone thinks, only that we're happy. Are you happy with the decision?"

"Yes…but what about Wynn?"

"Wynn is going to be fine. She'll come around, don't worry."

"Having the family gathered together to tell them all at once seemed a good idea when you set it up, but now it's so much pressure. What if things go awful? It could be a disaster."

"Then we ask them to leave. This isn't about them, it's our happiness that matters." He ran his thumb over her knuckles. "Stop worrying."

"Maybe you could take my mind off it." She licked her lips and wiggled her eyebrows. Having him naked again would keep her mind off the stress.

"Unless you want to make the announcement at a restaurant I should get dinner on."

"I'll help." She started to slide her legs off the sofa before he stopped her.

"Rest. I know you're tired, I'll get things started then I need to shower and change."

"I wouldn't be tired if you didn't keep me up all night." She paused, unable to stifle a yawn. "How you don't have circles under your eyes I don't know."

"The need for sleep was kicked out of me long ago." He leaned in and kissed her. "Everything is going to be fine, I promise."

When he headed to the kitchen, she let her head rest against the cushion of the sofa for a moment, and tried to gather her nerves. Being with Ace was what she wanted, what did she care if Wynn or the others weren't happy? What mattered was he made her happy. He was the man she had given her heart to years ago, and in a few months he would be her husband and a father to the child she carried. Things couldn't have worked out better if she had planned it.

Standing on the back deck, Ace cracked opened a beer bottle, watching the fall leaves scatter through the air.

Instead of giving him a second of peace, Lucky followed him. He rolled his shoulders and was ready to have it out with his brother. "Just get it out, so we can put this tension behind us. Though keep in mind nothing you say is going to change it. So you might want to keep your mouth shut and then I won't have to whoop your ass." He spun on his heels but instead of finding Lucky as he suspected, their father, Buck, stood there.

"Boy, I know you haven't lost your mind enough to speak to me that way." Even as a grown man, Buck's voice still managed to make him backtrack.

"Dad! I meant it for Lucky. I've already heard his input on my interest with Gwen, I thought he had returned for a second round."

"Lucky can wait. It's time you hear from me. I wasn't pleased with how you ended things with Gwen before."

"I know, but this time is different. I screwed up."

"Damn right you did and you broke your mother's heart in the process. Not to mention the state you left Gwen and the whole damn family."

"Dad..."

"I don't want to hear any excuses. I just want you to know if you screw this up again, you're going to have all of us wanting a piece of your ass. Gwen is a good girl, she deserves better than what you've done to her in the past. I'm damn surprised she didn't move on and find herself a good husband, someone who could treat her right." He glared at Ace, everything about the look reminding him just how angry his father was before. "You're not just getting a wife, but a child. You screw this up and you can find yourself a new family. Your mother and I raised you right, I won't have you disgracing the Diamond name." With that, Buck turned and walked back into the house.

"Well, that could have gone better." Ace leaned against the railing.

"What did you think would happen?" Lucky took a swig from his beer. "We were all left to put the pieces together while you were across the country living it up. Gwen could barely walk into the house with tears springing to her eyes."

"I know I fucked up before." With a clunk, he set his beer on the railing. "I failed her and the whole family, but not this time."

"For her sake I hope not." Lucky leaned against the railing, as cool as the air that whipped around them. "That's not why I came out here. I came to congratulate you."

"What?" He wasn't sure if he heard his brother correctly.

"Congratulations on getting your act together. Marrying Gwen might be the first thing you've done without your head up your ass and in your career. She's always loved you and now she's going to make an honest man out of you. I wish you both all the best." Lucky stepped away from the railing and headed for the door. "Don't screw this up."

Ace stood there alone with anger pulsing through him. He was tired of people thinking he was going to break Gwen's heart again. Did his family think so little of him? Sure, he had made his fair share of mistakes in the past, but he wasn't that bad of a person.

He had just polished off the last of his beer when Gwen opened the door. "I thought you were going to stick by my side tonight. Instead, I get trapped in the kitchen with Wynn. Your mom came to my rescue."

"Come here." He placed the empty beer bottle on the railing and held out his hand to her. She crossed the patio quickly. He wrapped his arms around her and pulled her against his chest. "I'm sorry for leaving you alone with Wynn, I just needed a breather. My family can be a bit intense."

"You're telling me."

"Do I need to have a talk with my baby sister?" He ran his hands down her back, enjoying the feel of her pressed against him.

"It's fine, she's just concerned. Your mom already had a few choice words for her. How did things go with Lucky and your dad?"

"Could have gone worse. Lucky congratulated me on getting my head out of my ass."

"Who'd have thought your mom would be the most supportive." She chuckled, sending the vibrations through him.

"I know you're upset Wynn isn't supportive too, but she'll come around. She's just worried her asshole brother is going to break your heart again."

"You won't," she whispered.

He kissed the top of her head. "I love you."

The love he had for her was stronger than anything he ever felt before. He wasn't about to mess it up.

"Look…" She pointed to the edge of the lawn. The moonlight was coming through the trees, casting a white, heart-shaped glow. "It's an omen."

"An omen of our love…It'll last through the darkest times and go on forever."

He lowered his head and claimed her lips.

Capturing a Diamond – SEALed for You

Explosive Passion

SEALed for You:
Book Two

Capturing a Diamond – SEALed for You

Navy SEAL Jared "Boom" Taylor is supposed to chaperone his best friend's sister home, but with a car malfunction and an impending storm, the plan goes out the window. Finding shelter in an abandoned cabin, with the one woman he can't get off his mind, is his chance to prove to her that military men are worth the added effort.

Boutique owner Wynn Diamond is on the verge of some exciting opportunities and with each new door opening things become more unnerving. Deciding to take refuge in a one-night stand to let off some steam, she never thought it would turn into more.

Could a one-night stand with a man in uniform actually be the forever she had been looking for?

Capturing a Diamond – SEALed for You

Chapter One

"Don't you dare!" Jared "Boom" Taylor slammed his hand on the steering wheel as the rental car sputtered to a stop on the side of the country road. This couldn't be happening. He had promised to get Wynn back to Virginia Beach. With the coughing and wheezing of the car, they weren't going anywhere.

"Boom?" Wynn Diamond, his best friend's baby sister, turned in the passenger seat to look at him. "What have you done?"

His lips curled up at the corner and he chuckled. "Why do women always assume the man did something when things go wrong?"

"You were driving."

He glanced down at the dashboard, rooting around for a hidden switch, anything that would reverse what she was claiming he did. His fingers ran over the smooth dashboard; he pushed against it looking for a hidden door with a switch. Yet he found nothing.

"What are you doing?" She raised an eyebrow at him, completely puzzled.

"Looking for this magical switch that you imply makes a car act like this." With a smirk, he glanced over at her. "I've been driving for years and I've never known there was one. Would you like to show me where it is?"

"Boom…"

"Or maybe you're saying before we left Ace and Gwen's wedding reception I tampered under the hood so that this would happen."

"With the farewell you put into action, no one would have missed you breaking the car," she teased.

When Ace asked Boom to be the best man, he gave him the stipulation that he wasn't to blow up anything during his wedding duties. As the SEAL Team Two's demolition expert, it wasn't possible for him not to do something that would create a loud boom to send the newlyweds off. It left him with only one course of action; he hired someone to do it for him. Lighting the evening sky with pink and white hearts was his way of giving the newlyweds a romantic farewell and keeping with his usual performance.

"I have to admit it was some send off." Her comment pulled him back from his amazing farewell.

"As best man it was my duty to send them off in style." He glanced over at Wynn in her pale blue bridesmaid's dress—he was sure it had a special name that only a woman would be able to tell him—her blonde shoulder-length hair pulled up, leaving only ringlets hanging down.

"At least you didn't blow up the place." She smirked at her smartass comment.

He had blown up plenty of buildings in the past but that wasn't a trip down memory lane he wanted to take. Placing his hand on the door handle, he peeled his gaze from her. "I'll see if I can fix this." He had to do something to get the car started again or she was going to freeze in that strapless dress as the temperatures plummeted.

He slipped out of the car, quickly closing the door behind him, and tugged his tuxedo jacket closed. The air had turned cold, announcing the storm that would soon be blanketing the area. It was rare for this part of Virginia to be hit with such a strong hurricane, but they had one barreling toward them that promised to be disastrous. If he didn't get the car going soon they'd have to find a place to bunker down. As the wind picked up he spotted a small cabin through the trees, maybe it would have a phone, because he knew his cell phone had no reception.

Every SEAL had to have basic mechanical skills, but propping open the hood he didn't have hope that it was something he could fix. What he needed was Bad Billy—a fellow SEAL—who could fix anything with an engine, but the rest of the team had stayed behind. They wanted to have a night to celebrate that the oldest of the team besides Lieutenant Commander Mac García had married.

Knowing the rest of the team was off partying while he had agreed to see Wynn home sent a twinge of jealousy though him.

Being the man he was Boom couldn't see Wynn traveling alone. When the youngest Diamond sibling, Lucky, announced he had to leave the wedding reception early for military duty; it left Boom to step up and escort her home.

Pushing it from his mind, he leaned under the hood and grabbed the dipstick to check the oil level. Nothing. There was just nothing on the dipstick. "You've got to be shitting me!"

The passenger door opened. "What is it?"

"We're not going anywhere." He waved the dipstick at her. "There's not a drop of oil in the bloody thing. Everything's jammed up because of it."

"What are we going to do?"

"Find a phone." He tipped his head in the direction he'd seen the cabin. "I'm going to see if I can find one there."

She glanced where he nodded. "I don't see anything."

"There's a cabin about a hundred feet from the road. Maybe there's a phone. I can call the rental car company and they can bring us a new car."

"It's nearly midnight. No one's going to bring us a new one now."

"Well, hopefully we can at least find somewhere warm, cause we'll freeze in the car." He moved around to the back of the car and opened the trunk.

"What are you doing?"

"If we're going to be stuck here tonight, I don't want to have to come back for your bag." He slipped it over his shoulder, before grabbing the jeans and sweater he wore earlier and a small box. "Why do women always pack so much?" he joked, pretending to do curls with the weight.

"Considering I came up two days before the wedding, I barely packed anything." She reached for the bag but he held it out of the way. "I'll take it if it's too heavy for the big SEAL."

Rolling his eyes, he slammed the trunk and headed for the trees. "Whatever you say."

"We can't go banging on someone's door at this time of night."

He paused just outside the line of trees. "Do you want to stay in the car and freeze?"

"No, but this dress and shoes aren't for walking through the woods." She pulled up the hem of her skirt and carefully stepped toward him.

"I could carry you."

"Thank you, but I'll pass on that." She stepped off the pavement and her heels sank a little into the ground beneath her feet. "You planned this, didn't you? You wanted me all to yourself and devised this car malfunction to do it," she teased. It was true they had spent much of the last few weeks together but even he wasn't as deceiving as that.

"Give me a little credit." His lips curled into a smile. "For a beautiful woman like you I would have planned it somewhere better than an abandoned cabin. We'd have broken down in front of a five-star resort or a beautiful cabin with amazing views. Something special that you'd never forget."

She paused, looking at him. Had he done something like that in the past? She shook her head, pushing the idea away. He was gorgeous and didn't need to do anything like that to get a woman into bed with him. She had no doubt that if he wanted them, they'd be lined up around the block waiting their turn. A twinge of jealousy coursed through her. She didn't want to think of other women in his bed. Instead, she glanced up at the cabin. "What if no one is there?"

"I don't think anyone's there. It looks abandoned." He slipped his arm lightly around her waist, making sure she was steady.

"We'll break in then?"

"They'll understand. We're miles from anywhere, nothing is in walking distance, and there won't be cars passing at this time of night. We have no other choice." He led her through the trees, bringing the cabin into view. It was a small one-story building, which looked to be well cared-for but empty for some time, like a vacation spot. *It was an odd place for a vacation home, but to each their own.*

As they crossed the empty space between road and cabin, the first raindrops began to fall. "Just what we need," he bitched.

"I love a good storm. We don't get nearly enough."

"Storms are fine, it's more the fact we need suitable shelter and heat before things pick up too badly." He was used to harsh conditions and could survive a night in the cold, but Wynn was another story. Ace would kill him if something happened to her. "Come along, let's get inside."

Chapter Two

The fire crackled, sending sparks up the chimney and heat through the room. Wynn stood in front of it with her hands outstretched, trying to chase the chill from her bones. The short walk from the car had frozen her to the bone. She had changed into her jeans but the only sweater she brought with her did very little to ease her discomfort.

For a day that had been so perfect this was a dramatic change. Going from a picture-perfect wedding to this abandoned cabin with a man she barely knew but lusted after. Before Ace and Gwen began planning their wedding, Wynn had only met Boom twice. In the last few weeks, they saw each other more regularly but for all purposes, he was still a stranger to her. A handsome stranger, and if he weren't her brother's best friend and a SEAL she might want to get to know him better. Naked better, that was.

The little tease of his hand around her waist as they made their way from the car only heated the fire within her. She wanted more of his gentle touch, to feel his hands on the most intimate parts of her body.

She shook her head, trying to push the thoughts away. She couldn't afford to think like that, especially not alone with him in a tiny cabin. It was too romantic with the glow of the fire and the wind and rain beating against the walls.

Boom came to stand next to her in front of the fire. "Here, this should warm you." He offered her a steaming cup of coffee.

"Where did you get this?"

"The box of stuff I carried from car." He took a sip from his own mug. "It was a few left over things from the wedding that your mom asked me to bring back. Coffee, a container of berries, some cookies, and left over favors."

"Great, we have coffee and cookies to survive on."

"We're not going to be here long enough to worry about needing food to survive." He sat the coffee on the mantel.

"How do you figure? There's no phone here, the car is dead; with this storm, how are we going to get out of here?" Desperation pitched her voice higher.

"Shhh…" He touched her shoulder. When she didn't move away, he pulled her into a hug. "I'll get us out of here. First light I'll set out for a phone."

"It could be miles away."

"I've gone longer in training, I'll make it wherever the phone is. We've just got to wait until morning. We're safe and warm here." His hand ran along her shoulder, drawing small circles against the fabric of her sweater. "I'll get you out of this mess and everything will be fine."

Her blood hot from his touch, she forced her gaze out the window, trying to cool her thoughts with the impending storm. Part of her wanted to press herself tighter against his ever-so-toned body, only to stop as thoughts of his career pushed their way into her mind.

Having her brother risk life and limb as a SEAL was enough; she sure didn't want her man doing it. She couldn't understand how Gwen was willing to stand by and have Ace risk everything, especially now that there was a child on its way. Her brother would be a father in less than two months. She thought maybe he'd leave the SEALs when his commitment was up and finally get a safe job, only to find out he had no intention of leaving his assignment and would re-up at the end of the year. What kind of life was that for Gwen and the baby? She shook her head. It wasn't a life she'd want. She wanted a man that would be there by her side.

He turned toward her, taking the coffee from her, setting it aside. She stood there, not sure what to do as his hand slid down her arm. His very touch was mesmerizing, keeping her locked in a trance watching him. It was that electricity that wouldn't let her go even if she wanted it to.

"I'm going to kiss you." Without giving her a moment to hesitate, he leaned into her and claimed her lips with his own. The spiciness from the coffee lingered on his lips, mixing with her vanilla lip-gloss. He used his tongue to gently ease her mouth open, giving him entrance and allowing their tongues to dance together. She leaned closer, her hand traveling up his chest; he kissed her one final time before pulling back.

When she finally regained herself, she stepped out of his embrace. "We shouldn't have done that."

"Why not?"

"Which reason should I give you, because I have a few?" When he didn't answer, she continued. "You're a SEAL, and I never get involved with military men. Not to mention Ace would have a fit; you're his best friend."

"Shouldn't that be a good thing? Then he'd know his baby sister was in good hands."

"I don't get involved with military men," she repeated, more determined than before. Only this time, she wasn't sure if she was trying to convince him or herself.

"Make an exception and it won't be something you regret." He advanced toward her, closing the distance she had put between them only seconds before. "We're here together for a reason."

"Yeah, because the car broke down," she reminded him.

"I've always believed things happen for a reason." He laid a hand on her forearm. "Rental cars go through inspections every time they come in. I didn't see a leak when I pulled it from the hotel parking lot. For it to have seized up the engine as it did means there's no oil left in the whole damn thing, yet it made it to the hotel just fine yesterday."

"Are you saying someone did this to get us stranded together? They could have got us killed."

He shook his head. "Not someone, but maybe a something. A master plan, a God, whatever you believe."

"After everything you've seen, how can you believe there's something beyond what we can see with the naked eye?"

"How can I not? I've been in positions I never thought I'd make it out of, yet somehow I did. I believe there's been something that has kept me and the rest of the team safe. Otherwise I wouldn't still be here."

Unable to fathom that he believed in a higher being, she took a step back and perched herself on the armrest of the sofa. "You're the team's demolition expert; I've heard stories of things blowing up all around you, including IED's, and still you come away untouched."

"That's why I believe." He shoved his hands into the pockets of his jeans. "I've seen so many lose a body part or worse, their lives because of IED's, yet I've survived. There has to be a reason that I'm still here; some great purpose."

"Right there is the reason I don't get involved with military men." He stared at her as if he didn't understand. "There's too much risk involved with your job. It's bad enough worrying about Ace and Lucky every time they're deployed. I don't need another man in my life to worry about."

"So you'd rather play it safe and not love?" He raised an eyebrow.

"Safe isn't a bad thing, and as for love I'm open to it for someone with a safe job. You're not safe." She dragged her hand through her hair sprayed thick hair, tugging the blonde locks away from her face.

"Fine, not long-term. What about tonight?"

"Tonight." The word came out on a whisper. In that moment to have even just one night with him sounded like paradise. It would be the first time she lived on the edge instead of just playing things by the book. Designing the specialty stuff she carried in her little boutique just off the boardwalk took all her time. There was nothing left over for a relationship, leaving her lonely.

Giving into the flirtation that had been playing them for weeks, she nodded. "Tonight…only."

Chapter Three

Boom couldn't keep the smirk off his face. Since he began spending time with her during the wedding planning, he couldn't keep his thoughts off her. This one night he was going to make it turn into much more. It might be his only shot with her and he wasn't going to let it slip past. If he was going to convince her that this could work, he was going to have a fight on his hands; one that might be the worst he'd ever experienced in all his years in the military. Though he had a feeling Wynn Diamond was a woman worth fighting for.

"I've found blankets in the closet; I'll make us a bed in front of the fire and we'll open the bottle of wine I brought." He winked at her before strolling toward where he found the blankets.

"I'll get the wine."

"It's on the counter." He tipped his head to the other side of the cabin, where a bar divided the kitchen and living room. While she went for the wine he went down the short hallway that led to the only bedroom and bathroom.

Minutes later, he had a makeshift bed spread out before the fire. With no heat besides what came from the fireplace, they had no other option but to make a bed on the floor if they wanted to stay warm. With all the blankets he could find, and pillows from the bed spread out he turned back to her.

"Last chance to change your mind." There would be no going back from this. She was going to be his.

"I want you…even if it's only for one night." She handed him the glass of wine before taking a sip out of her own glass.

Not wanting to spoil the mood, he took a sip of his wine before setting it aside and keeping quiet. There was no reason to argue about the one night comment now. "You're beautiful. Come." He pulled her toward the fireplace.

They eased down onto the blankets and he pressed his lips to hers softly. Letting each new kiss explore a little deeper, until the passion between them ignited like the fire they sat in front of. Their tongues danced together, giving him the taste of the wine on her lips, and the air sizzled around them. There was enough heat between them to warm the place without the fire.

Their time together in this special place was short and he didn't want to miss a second of it. He broke their kiss to lift her sweater over her head. "You have too many clothes on."

"You too." She grabbed the waist of his sweater and pulled it off.

"Lay back." As she did what he asked, he let his hands slide down her curves until he unbuttoned her jeans and pulled them slowly down her legs. The sexy pale blue panties that matched her bra called to him, he grabbed them with his teeth and pulled them away. Laying her bare sent desire racing through him. No longer able to control himself, he slid the panties off the rest of the way before easing her legs open.

She leaned forward, dragging her hand over his head, fingers sliding over his buzz cut. He pushed her back gently, making her lay flat once again, and pressed his lips to her stomach. He kissed around her bellybutton, grazing his teeth along her tender flesh. He stroked her thighs with his fingertips, until with every touch she arched into him, demanding more. Nudging her legs further apart, his fingers delved inside her and she met the teasing thrusts eagerly. A demanding moan vibrated through her body. Passion drove his hand harder and faster.

The trail of wicked kisses tingled over the insides of her thighs. He slipped his fingers from her, quickly replacing them with his mouth, while his hands moved to her hips, holding her against him as she wiggled in desire. Tiny nips and gentle licks flicked over her sweet spot, nearly driving her over the edge. "Boom!" Her fingernails dug into his shoulders until he could feel the skin break and blood trickle from the tiny moon shapes.

"I want you...please, Jared!" The way she called out his given name made it more intimate. It had been a very long time since someone called him anything but Boom.

He slid up her body until he hovered over her. With one hand, he unhooked the front clasp of her black lace bra, baring her completely to him. "Damn, you're beautiful!" He trailed wet, teasing kisses to each of her hard dusky pink nipples. Drawing one into his mouth, he let his tongue circle around it, before grazing his teeth along it and letting it slip from his mouth, moving to the other one.

"Please…" That one simple word, deeply laced with desire, sped his pace.

"Anything for you, Wynn." He pulled away long enough to shed the rest of his clothes. Her gaze scorched as it swept over him. "Do you like what you see, beautiful?"

"Maybe," she said coyly.

"Humm, just maybe? Let's see what we can do about that." Confidence and cockiness surged through him. He lowered himself, careful to stay just above her.

"Please, I want you now."

"What's the rush? We have all night."

"Then give it to me now, and we can have another round or two later." There was a twinkle in her eye.

"Mmm, a woman after my own heart." He placed his hands gently on her thighs, spreading them further, giving him the access that he desired. He teased her sensitive flesh with his fingers before finally sliding himself in to her warm wet core until he filled her completely. A cry of desire and need escaped her lips. Her body arched and she nibbled the side of his neck.

Her moans of pleasure spurred him faster. His hips increased pace, driving forcefully into her with each thrust. Their bodies, bound together, found a rhythm; passion shot through him, made him desperate for release. He fought the ecstasy, fought to hang on and drive her to climax. Digging her nails into his back, she writhed. Their lips met again and again. She screamed against his mouth and he held on for another few seconds, prolonging the beautiful agony until finally reaching release.

He knew he wanted more of her, doubted he would ever get enough. He collapsed next to her, their legs entwined, his energy spent for the moment. She curled her body into his, her hand resting on his chest.

"Looks as though you enjoyed that, beautiful." He wrapped his arms around her.

"Oh yes." She lazily ran a hand up and down his chest. "Ready for another round?"

He snickered. "I'm a SEAL; I'm always ready."

Capturing a Diamond – SEALed for You

Chapter Four

The fire cast a faint glow over the room as it began to die down, as the fire died so did their need, leaving behind exhaustion. Wynn lay cuddled against Boom's body, her hand lying across his chest, holding him close while her mind screamed for her to run. Giving in to desire for one night with him was supposed to relieve her longing for him. Instead, it already wasn't enough. She wanted more.

No! One night, that's it. She wouldn't put herself through what she witnessed so many military spouses suffer through. It was no life worrying that he wouldn't come home, or waiting by the phone for him to call, or at the computer for an email. That wasn't something she could do. She needed a man who would be there with her, by her side, not off fighting against things that go bump in the night.

She had done one-night stands in the past and each time it released sexual tension, rejuvenated her, and allowed her to put sex on the back burner for the time. With Boom, it did the complete opposite: she wanted more of him in every way.

"What's on your mind?" His fingers rubbed down her arm.

"This isn't how it's supposed to work."

"What isn't?"

"This." She forced herself to stop tracing the lines of his abs and leaned up on her elbow. "One-night stands; it's about sex and then both people go about their lives. They don't lay here and cuddle."

"What would you prefer? We each go to our own place in the cabin? Maybe I sleep in the kitchen?" He smirked. "But if I may say something without making you angry…you were the one cuddling with me."

"What?" Surprised, she raised an eyebrow at him, but realized he was right and went to pull away.

"Not that I'm complaining, but your naked body was pressed against mine." He closed the distance she had put between them. "You're the one that said tonight only, not me."

Pressing her back against the corner of the sofa, the wood digging into her skin, she tried to ground herself. "You agreed."

"Only that I'd have you tonight."

"You conceded, bastard!" She tried to pull the blanket from him so she could get up without baring her nakedness to him again.

"I asked you before to let me show you what I could give you. Tonight was the first part and I'm not giving up now. What are you so afraid of?"

She let her head fall back against the cushion, trying to figure out the best way to answer his question. She wanted to tell him she wasn't afraid, but that wasn't the case, she was terrified she'd give him her heart and he wouldn't come back.

"Living here, surrounded by so many military families, dealing with Ace and Lucky's careers, I'm all too aware of the dangers."

"Ace and I were made for this, it's what we've wanted all our lives. Nothing's going to happen to us."

"Bullshit." She squared her shoulders, refusing to let her emotions control her. "One of the missions could be the last, leaving me heartbroken and alone. I can't do that."

"Yet, yesterday you stood by while your best friend did that very thing, and you gave her your blessing."

"Ace is a stubborn man. He'll come back to her. He wouldn't let some terrorist stand between him and Gwen, not now when they just found each other again." Jealousy teased through her with the knowledge that Gwen and Ace had something that she wanted, but was denying herself. *No, Boom isn't the right one. Someday the right man will come and I'll have it too.*

"As would I." He placed his hand over hers. "We do this job to protect America, to keep you safe, to allow our children to be born into a world where they don't have to fear what might happen. We want to make this country safe, so that we don't have a repeat of nine-eleven or any of the other disasters that have happened. Don't you want your niece to be brought into a world where she can live free and safe?"

"I get why you do it and I admire it. Ace, Lucky, you and the rest are my heroes. You risk yourself so that others can enjoy life without truly understanding the dangers that surround us." She reached out and cupped his cheek. "I just don't want my heart broken."

He tipped his head into her hand and kissed her palm. "Sweet cheeks, I'm not going to break your heart."

Everything in her wanted to believe his words. She wanted to believe that he'd always come back to her, no matter what he faced, but it scared the hell out of her.

"Wynn, I've never wanted a woman the way I want you—like a lit match in a powder magazine. Give us a chance."

"I can't." She tugged the blanket tight against her. "I need a man who will be there; one I can snuggle against each night. Being with a military man is like being single half the time."

"But the other half is like being newlyweds. It makes up for any time away."

"It's not like you're normal military, where you deploy for six months to a year. Your deployment rotation is faster than other branches; even when you're not deployed, you're still not actually home. Most of your training isn't done here." She glanced toward the fire. "You're just gone too much."

"That's not something I can change but the time we're together will be unbelievable." He ran the back of his finger along her jawline. "Wouldn't that make up for what time I'm gone?"

"Please, Jared…you're an amazing man, but I just can't." She shook her head over and over, as if it would solidify the decision in her heart.

"I'm not going to stop fighting for you."

Unable to handle it any longer she slipped past him, grabbed her clothes, and headed to the bathroom. She needed to get away from him before he wore down her resistance further. Tears sprang to her eyes, and she fought to keep them from falling. *I can't do this…not with him.*

Capturing a Diamond – SEALed for You

Chapter Five

After getting dressed, Wynn snuck out the back of the house. With nowhere else to go, she stood on the small porch at the back of the cabin, trying to gather herself. The sex had been amazing, better than she could have hoped for, and that's what made it so much harder. She wanted what Gwen had. She longed for and searched for it, but had never found it.

In the past few weeks of actually getting to know Boom, one amazing evening of sex and she couldn't get him off her mind. He could give her everything she wanted, except himself; that, she'd only get part-time. The military would always have the other half. All these years she said she wouldn't make that sacrifice. She already did when it came to her brothers, she wouldn't do it with her husband. Now for the first time she wondered if her rule was standing in the way of her happiness.

Could a relationship with Boom really work, even with him gone so often? Or would resentment at being left alone eventually set in? Between designing the latest fashions for her boutique and running the shop, she was busy. She needed a man who would understand her creative whims and wouldn't fuss if she spent all night in her studio or slipped out of bed in the middle of the night because an idea came to her that she had to get down on paper.

The future could get even more hectic with the latest offer she received. Just three days before the wedding she got the offer of a lifetime. Not wanting to steal the spotlight from Ace and Gwen, she kept it to herself. Plus, it was best to wait until the ink dried on the contract before official announcements were shared. Then they could really celebrate, before the real work set in.

She shook her head as the realization of what she wanted sank in. It wasn't fair that she expected her man to accept her career when she couldn't accept his. If he was military and she cared for him, then she should accept it. How could she expect someone to do it for her if she wasn't willing to do it for them? Relationships were give and take, if she wanted to explore where things could go with Boom she'd have to accept his choice of careers.

"It's too cold for you to be out here without something warmer on." He wrapped a blanket around her shoulders.

She took hold of the blanket so it wouldn't fall onto the wet porch and turned to face him. "I didn't hear you come out."

"I came around the front, because I checked the car first. When I didn't find you in the bathroom I thought you'd taken refuge in the car out of the howling wind."

"I didn't even think about it." The wind picked up and her body shivered against the assault. "I just needed a few minutes to get my thoughts together."

"I figured. You've been out here twenty minutes. It's time to come in before you catch your death. If you want me to stay in the car, I will."

"What makes you think I can't handle the cold but you can?" Her sadness turned to anger, and it showed in her voice.

"It's cold but not the worst weather I've had to deal with by far. I'd survive." He held up his hand, stopping her as she started to say something. "This has nothing to do with you being a woman, so don't pull that card with me. You've never had to deal with the shit I have, my body is used to it. I barely feel the cold any longer. Now, please come inside."

With one last glance up at the darkening sky, she nodded. "I wouldn't make you sleep in the car."

"I never thought you would, but I offered." He laid his hand on the small of her back and led her to the door. "I didn't mean to upset you."

Stepping into the warmth, she realized how cold she was. Her teeth chattered and her hands shook. "Come sit with me by the fire." Too cold to wait to see if he followed, she dashed forward to the warmth of the fireplace.

Without a word, he followed her, keeping a little bit of distance between them. He sat down on the chair furthest from the fire.

Damn did he look fine sitting there like he didn't have a care in the world! The heather gray sweater was pulled tight across his chest, showing off the contours of his abs, and she wanted to run her hands over them again. She forced herself to stay where she was, her gaze on the fireplace away from his perfect body.

"Outside I realized something…" She took a deep breath and forced herself to continue. "I work crazy hours, sometimes all night or for days at a time, only crashing for an hour or two. If I expect someone to accept that then I should be willing to accept their job. Don't get me wrong, your job is dangerous and I don't like it, but I should at least try."

"What are you saying, Wynn?"

"I don't know what's between us or where it could go but I could try to explore it." She glanced back at him. "The occasional times I've seen you I've always wished you weren't a SEAL, then I could allow more than just indulging in flirtation. These past few weeks while we've been helping to plan the wedding for Gwen and Ace I've seen a whole different side to you, one that goes deeper than flirtation; I want the chance to explore it, to see where it could lead."

He leaned forward, his elbows on his knees. "I told you before I'm not going to stop fighting for you. If you take this next step you better be ready for the real thing."

She swallowed the lump that had formed in her throat. "I guess I am."

"I'm not saying it's going to be easy, and some days are going to be an uphill battle. You might even ask yourself why the hell you're doing it. However, I promise you that every chance I get I'm going to prove to you how amazing things can be between us. On the bad days I want you to remember all the good times we have together."

"I'll try." Her heart raced and doubts rushed through her mind. *I must be crazy, breaking my one rule for relationships.*

"Doubting yourself already?" She glanced at him, her eyebrow raised, and he added. "Your body went rigid. It's a clear-cut sign of doubt or fear. In your case, I think both."

"Maybe a little, but didn't you say you'd make it worth it?" she taunted.

"I did." He stretched his long legs out in front of him and rose.

"Where are you going?"

"Wedding snacks. Get comfortable, I'm going to make this a night you won't forget."

The way the words rolled off his tongue made her wonder what he had in mind. With her sweater falling to just past her upper thigh, she slipped out of her damp jeans and back onto the makeshift bed. She'd make tonight count and take tomorrow as it came. Ace's words echoed in her head. *Tomorrow's never guaranteed...*

Capturing a Diamond – SEALed for You

Chapter Six

Not taking any risks with the one chance he had to eliminate the doubt he saw in Wynn's eyes, he grabbed the open bottle of wine and a plastic container of strawberries and raspberries. Tonight he was going to show her all the positive things he could offer, because without a doubt the negatives would be rearing their ugly heads soon enough. The better he could show her how things would be when he was there, the less she'd doubt what was happening between them. At least that's what the logical part of him said. The rest of him just wanted to get her naked again.

Closing the distance to her, he chuckled. He was falling for a woman that wouldn't be just another fling. Only a short time ago he tried to sway Ace from getting involved with Gwen. The situation might have been different but still set forth the same results; the only difference was the child that Ace and Gwen were expecting in less than a month. *Oh how the mighty have fallen to the wiles of women.* He smirked and pushed the thoughts aside, his attention falling where it deserved to be: on the amazing Wynn.

"What do you have there?" She smoothed the blanket around her hips.

"Berries and champagne would have been better but wine will have to do in a pinch." He topped off her glass before setting the bottle on the end table. "I'm going to feed you strawberries and we're going to talk."

"Talk?" Surprise laced her voice.

"Yes. Though we've run into each other for years at parties Ace threw, or family events he invited me to, and over the last several weeks planning the wedding, we've never really gotten to know each other. So let's start there, and then, well, I have other plans before the night is over." He took hold of the stem of the first strawberry. "You said before that your business takes a lot of your time, tell me about it."

"Roll of the Diamond, it's a little fashionable boutique just off the boardwalk. We only sell my designs there. It's not huge, but it's what I love doing. We also do custom orders, like Gwen's wedding dress and my bridesmaid dress. The custom orders extend from everything to shirts, pants, a whole wardrobe, or even wedding attire."

"I can see the passion in your eyes when you speak of the boutique. You love your work just as I love mine." He dangled a strawberry in front of her lips, waiting for her to take a bite.

"I know." She leaned just a little forward, lips closing around the strawberry; some of the rich juices drizzled down the corner of her mouth.

Without thinking about it, he ran his finger from her chin up to the corner of her lip to catch the liquid and licked his finger. Their gazes locked while she ate the last half of the berry.

"I know you could never be anything other than what you are. You're a SEAL; it's not just your job, it's you, down to the very core. I know the dedication you have because I've seen it in Ace. You both are two of the same coin."

He took a raspberry from the dish and popped it in his mouth. "I hadn't planned to bring my work up tonight."

"But it seeps in." She took the raspberry he offered. "That's what the military does. It affects every aspect of your life, making everything else fold around it in order to survive."

"I'm seeing those doubts again."

"Actually, just the opposite." She took a long sip of the wine. "Unlike Gwen, I didn't grow up with the military, but I have seen how it affects a life because of my brothers. Things can never be planned because deployments or training can come up; holidays and family events are missed for the same reasons. In a way, my life is just as complicated. I don't deploy at a moment's notice as you do, but the boutique demands everything of me. Maybe this type of relationship is one that can suit us both."

"What's that supposed to mean?"

"We're both busy and enjoy our work, but it limits what we have to give to someone else. Taking this as it might be, and cherishing the moments we have together… There's no reason we both can't be devoted to what we love and still have time together. I have a feeling those times would be magical all on their own."

"Oh my beautiful Wynn, they will be magical, but as I told you before I'm in this for the long run. I'm not going to be satisfied with brief encounters when our ships pass in the night and I don't think you will be either."

"How do you know what I'd be satisfied with?" She set the wineglass aside and moved up against the pillows. "I've done one-night stands and flings and they work for me. Boyfriends can't understand my work obsession, even ones who are as dedicated to their profession. Too many of them see my designs as a hobby, not a business, but damn it, Roll of the Diamond is more than just a hobby or a way to make a living. It's what I do, and making a living is a lot more than just what my boutique can do."

"Wow, Wynn, I meant no…"

"No, I'm the one that's sorry." She dragged her fingers through her hair. "I love my business, but my mother just thinks it's a hobby. Now that Ace has married and there's a granddaughter on the way, she thinks I should be next. Give up my boutique, settle down and become a baby machine. That's not me."

"I never said it was." He laid his hand on her arm, smoothing up and down it. "Your family always seemed supportive."

"My parents are supportive of Ace and Lucky, but the hidden secret is that they hate my work. My designs are too edgy and revealing; they want me to close up shop and settle down with a nice man who can take care of me. That's not me. I'm not Suzie homemaker who's happy being barefoot and pregnant. I want a life and a career of my own. Why should I have to choose?"

"You shouldn't. You can have everything you want and be married, even have some munchkins if that's what you want."

He hated to see her so frustrated. The very idea that her parents pressured her to give up something she loved ate at his stomach. He had been there with his own parents, and in the end it only made things tense between them. A trip home hadn't happened in years, even phone calls to his parents were effectively nonexistent between because of the tension over his choice of careers. He didn't like the idea that Wynn was suffering with the same thing. Maybe he'd talk with Ace and they'd see if the two of them could make the Diamond parents lay off of Wynn's career choice.

Capturing a Diamond – SEALed for You

Chapter Seven

Discussing her family and their views on her boutique made Wynn's stomach churn. All her life she'd strived for her parent's approval. The boutique was the first thing that was really against what they wanted for her. It was the one thing she wanted more than anything else was and she wasn't about to give it up.

"Three days ago I received a call from New York. I kept it to myself because I knew what my parents' reaction would be and I didn't want to spoil the wedding." She paused, unable to refuse when he dangled another strawberry in front of her.

"What did they want?" He pushed as she enjoyed the sweet berry.

"Me…well, my designs." She swallowed, pushing the anxiety down. "I have seven days to prepare ten designs for them to evaluate. If they like them, I'll have a small section in a boutique on Fifth Avenue in New York City."

"That's wonderful, congratulations!" He leaned forward and pressed his lips to hers. The wine lingered on his lips, mixing with the berries to provide an alluring combination. Wanting more, she slipped her tongue between his lips, allowed them to dance for a moment before pulling away.

"I've been dying to tell someone. I tried to get Lucky alone so I could tell him yesterday but he was so busy with last minute details and then the bachelor party. Ace and Gwen won't know until they get back from their honeymoon and I didn't want to tell my parents until things were official because I knew how they'd react." She was rambling but it felt like a weight was lifted off her chest. Finally, someone knew, and better still, they actually celebrated it with her.

"How about when we make it back home, I cook you dinner and we'll celebrate?"

"You don't have to do that." The kindness of his offer touched her.

"I want to, and don't you worry sweet cheeks, I know how to cook. What do you say? Will you join me for dinner? We'll make it back home tomorrow and I know you're itching to get back to work, so how about the next night?"

"Okay." She nodded, because dinner was the next step in seeing where what was between them could go.

"Good." He held out another berry. "I hate to be the one to press a sore subject but when are you going to tell your parents?"

"As much as I would love to hear their support, I won't get it, so I'm going to wait as long as I can. I'm sure one of my big-mouthed brothers will say something about it before I get around to it. There's no reason to fight them if I don't get it, so I'll wait, and *if* I get the contract for the space in New York then I'll deal with them."

"I'm sorry they're not more supportive." He cupped her hand between his two larger ones. "I know it's hard because I've been there."

"Ace told me that you've lost contact with your family."

Deep sadness fogged his face. "They don't care for my career. If I'm willing to give it up then I can be included back in the family fold, otherwise…"

"I'm sorry." His pain cut deep within her. Her family would never disown her, at least she hoped not, over her life choices.

"As you said before, being a SEAL is who I am; I can't change, not even for my family. They chose not to accept me for who I am and I have to live with it." He lifted her hand to his lips, gently laying a kiss on her knuckles. "I hope you won't make the same mistake they did."

"I won't." Their families' disapproval wasn't the first thing they had in common, but might very well be the strongest. "Ace mentioned before you have a younger brother, do you have any contact with him?"

"Not much. Once he turned eighteen, I thought things would change but he was in college. With our parents paying his tuition, he must obey their rules or the finances would be cut off, but even after that nothing changed." His thumb ran over her knuckles, gently caressing them. "None of that matters. The designs you need to send, do you have them done?"

"Not yet. I have some designs on my desk at home. They've been lined up for the coming seasons, but I'm not sure any of them are good enough for New York. I have a young girl, Melody, who works in the boutique. She's going to pick up a few extra hours so I can have some more time to design. Ideas are already running around in my head like demented mice, I just need to sketch them out. Once I get to work it won't be long, well, that is if I can settle on the ideas that are best for this."

"You'll find the perfect ones to blow them away," he reassured her. "I know next to nothing about the fashion world, but do you have to make the clothes yourself too? Can you do that in ten days?"

"All I have to do now is sketch them out. If they like my work, whatever ones they choose we'll design and ship to New York. I have an in-house person who does all the actual sewing. I could do it, and did when the shop first opened, but now I focus more on the designing while still keeping a hand on the other parts." She rubbed her hand along his cheek, the start of stubble pushing through his skin met her touch. "Thank you."

"For what?"

"Asking about my work. I know it's not your thing so it means a lot to me that you let me ramble on about it." When he started to say something she ran her forefinger over his lips, only to have him suck it into his mouth. "When you're not busy with the military what do you like to do?" The question came out breathier than she had planned, full of need, while his tongue circled the tip of her finger.

"A little of this and that. I enjoy being on the water, so I have a boat. It's not much but it allows me to get out there and do what I want. It has a small cabin, mostly a bedroom, but there's a small kitchen, so if I want to stay out on the water for days at a time I can."

"I haven't been on the water in years. The closest I seem to get any more is the view from my condo." She tried to joke about it, but couldn't quite finish it off with a smile. "This trip is showing me more than I wanted."

He sat his glass aside, moved up next to her, and wrapped his arm around her shoulders. "Sometimes we need a little wake-up call so we don't miss the life we were given. Too bad we can't give our parents theirs and then maybe they'd stop doubting our career choices."

"Do you ever have times when you doubt yourself? That maybe you put too much time into your career?" She shook her head before he could answer. "I guess you wouldn't. The military decides how much time you do."

"The military decides some, yes, but there's always ways for a SEAL to go above and beyond. Our team has volunteered for missions when it wasn't our turn and we do more training than others because Lieutenant Commander Mac García likes to whip us into shape when we leave off a little too much steam." He squeezed her tight against the line of his body. "You put extra time in when you love your job, there's nothing wrong with that as long as you take the time to enjoy life. One thing the military taught me is to live every day to the fullest. We're going to do that. Once the weather is nice and you've signed that big New York contract, we're going to go out on my boat for a few days, just the two of us, and celebrate."

"That sounds ideal. I can only imagine the sunsets when surrounded by nothing but water. It will be the perfect way to celebrate but I'll only go if you promise to make love to me under the stars. It's something I've always wanted to do."

"I can do that, but first I'll make love to you in front of this fireplace again, right now." He reached around her, putting his hand on her hip farthest from him, and tugged her into his lap so that she was straddling him.

"A bit of an assumption that I want you, isn't it?"

"No." He nuzzled her neck, placing little kisses along its curve. "Your body screams your desires. You want me as much as I want you."

Chapter Eight

The coldness of the cabin pulled Wynn from a deep sleep. Keeping her eyes closed, she enjoyed the sensation of being cuddled against the warmth of Jared's body, his arm still holding her tight. For the first time she realized there was nothing better than waking up next to someone you cared about. It was pure heaven, but something besides the dying fire had woken her.

She opened her eyes to find cowboy boots caked with mud and debris just off to the side of the makeshift bed. Her gaze traveled up the boots to find an older gentleman with a shotgun pointed at them.

"Jared!" The alarm in her voice woke him from his slumber.

His eyes flew open to the old man and he sat up, using his body as a barrier between her and the shotgun. "What do you want? Money? My wallet's on the end table, take whatever you want."

"I don't want your money. You're trespassing. I want you and your woman out of here." The man tipped his head toward the door.

"Our rental car broke down last night as we were traveling home from a wedding. With no cell phone reception, we needed shelter for the night. At first light I was prepared to set out and find a phone. I must have overslept," Jared explained.

"The nearest cabin is seven miles, you wouldn't have made it. That's your car on the road?" As the old man put the pieces together, he lowered the gun slightly. It was enough to allow her to breathe a little easier, knowing they weren't about to be shot.

"I'm a Navy SEAL. The distance wouldn't have been an issue," he assured the older man. "The name's Jared Taylor, but everyone calls me Boom, and this is Wynn. We apologize for intruding, but your cabin was all we could find."

"It's not mine. I watch it, since the owners only use it for hunting." He pointed the gun at the floor, no longer seeing them as threat. "I'll wait outside while you two get dressed and then I'll take you to a phone. You can call for a replacement car."

"Thank you." Her voice was mild, her heartbeat finally slowing after being scared nearly to death.

When the door shut behind him, she collapsed back onto the pillows. "Shit."

"Your mom would wash your mouth out with soap if she heard you cursing." He leaned over her, his hands sliding under his sweater, which she had put on before they had fallen asleep. "It's a good thing you got chilly, or he'd have found us both naked. At least mine would have been hidden."

"Next time I'll make sure to steal the covers then," she teased as he stood up, baring his nakedness. "Umm and what a wonderful body he'd have seen."

He grabbed his boxers and jeans from by the fireplace and started to get dressed. "Something tells me he wouldn't have enjoyed it as much as you."

"No, I don't think he would have, but I do." She held out her hands and he laid her clothes in her open grip. "I want to see a lot more of it once we are back in Virginia Beach."

"I was hoping you'd say that. Now, off with my sweater so I can clean up these blankets." She tugged her boot-cut jeans up her legs and zippered them before letting him pull his sweater over her head. His fingers ran along her sides, teasing over her hips before making their way to the sides of her breasts. "Sweet cheeks, I had planned to make love to you again this morning but maybe you'll give me a chance once we get back to your condo."

"I think we can come to some terms." The chill of the cabin had her nipples hardening, sending desire through her as if they were a direct line to her core. "I need to get dressed, it's chilly."

She gathered the rest of her clothes from where they were tossed, quickly dressing before helping him fold the blankets. Sadness clung to them, neither of them wanting their little escape to end. Now they had to get back to the real world and see if things could actually work between them or if it was just a pipe dream.

It was funny how life could change in less than twenty-four hours, and how her vow to avoid military men like the plague could suddenly seem so pointless. In a few words, Jared had a way of making her see reality, rather than what she wanted to. He was a man she wanted both in her life and in her bed.

Night had fallen long before Boom pulled the new rental car into a parking spot in front of Wynn's building. Any hope of arriving early and spending some quality time with her, maybe even enjoying a quiet dinner, some wine, and a romp in the hay were dashed when it took six hours for the rental agency to bring them a new car.

He was tired, but more importantly he was in desperate need of a shower. Food seemed overrated, but sex he'd never pass up with Wynn. He couldn't get that woman off his mind, images of her naked ran through his head like a private porno twenty-four/seven.

"I know the other members of your team were going out to celebrate last night and make it a long weekend, so I really appreciate you bringing me home." Her words pulled him from his thoughts as he shoved the gearshift into park.

"It was the best decision I've made. I didn't plan on the car malfunctioning and I know it held you back from the work you wanted to do, but spending that night at the cabin… I wouldn't change it for anything." He slipped out of the car before she could say anything and dashed to open the passenger door.

"Will you stay?"

He looked into her eyes, seeing the mix of emotions, before shaking his head. She was so easy to read, her eyes gave her away. She wanted to work but also wanted him to stay. "Tonight you'll work and rest. Then tomorrow I'll pick you up at seven for a late dinner and either I'll come back to your place or you can come to mine, but I want you in my arms again."

"Thank you. I am excited to get to work, but I'll miss you tonight."

He slipped his arm around her waist. "Me too, but tomorrow when we're both well-rested and you've had time to get some of your ideas down on paper, it will be better." With a light kiss, he grabbed her bag from the trunk.

They strolled toward the main door of her condo building, his arm around her waist. "How about I cook tomorrow? We have a quiet dinner here and dessert in bed where I can eat it off your chest."

"That sounds better than going out." The attendant opened the door and stepped back to give them room to enter. "All these years and I've never known we are practically neighbors. I'm two condo buildings down, and from my place you can see where my boat is tied."

Being back in Virginia Beach made things more serious between them. It wouldn't be long before his work started to interfere with plans, or Ace found out that his best friend was in a relationship with his sister, or one of a million other things that could interfere came up. *No, this is about us, no one else. I won't let them interfere.*

Capturing a Diamond – SEALed for You

Chapter Nine

W eeks flew by with only a few uphill battles but somehow they made it through everything thrown at them. The biggest threat had been Wynn's brother, who she had done her best to deal with, though she suspected Boom was still dealing with it since he had to work with Ace on a near-daily basis. The one thing she had been worried about from the start, the SEAL duties, hadn't become an issue *yet.* Since he was home now, there were no deployments on the horizon, and training happening at their home base, she wasn't concerned with it at the moment. That could change at any moment, so she took advantage of what she could control.

Carrying cupcakes from Boom's favorite bakery in town, she strolled through the lobby of his condo building and up to the elevator. It was becoming a second home to her. If they didn't end up in her bed, they were in his. Since the wedding, they had only spent a handful of nights apart.

"Hold that elevator, sweet cheeks." She had just stepped into the elevator as he came jogging toward her in his camouflaged blue-gray Navy working uniform.

"You're supposed to be upstairs, waiting for our afternoon romp in the sack. Remember, you're the one that said you had an early day and we'd have the whole weekend, so I got Melody to cover the shop so I could spend it with you." She put her hand on her hip and waited for an answer, when all she wanted to do was push him against the elevator wall and have her way with him. *Damn does he look good in uniform!*

"I got hung up with your brother. He's invited us over for dinner on Sunday, our godchild would like to see us."

"Our godchild." She held her hand out to him. "Give me your cell phone, I've got to call the papers and news stations."

"What?" He dug into his pocket and produced his phone.

"If that month-old niece of mine is talking then we're all going to be rich and famous." She laughed at her own smart-ass comment. "I smell a set-up. How much do you want to bet Ace is determined to have one of his *chats* about this relationship and Gwen's doing it at the house so she can control how things go and try to nip my overprotective brother in the ass before he gets out of hand?"

"I could practically guarantee it." He shoved the phone back in his pocket and took a step forward to open the box she held. "Yum."

"Not until after you've changed and had lunch." She moved the box to the side before he could reach in and grab one of the cupcakes.

"I was hoping to have you for lunch." He placed his hands on her hips, gliding them up slowly.

"Maybe that's what I meant." Before she could act on her urge to have him right there, the elevator doors opened.

"Damn, if I'd have known I'd have had you right here." With his hand in hers, he stepped out of the elevator and took her with him. "I've thought of nothing but this weekend together all week. Just me and you, in the middle of nowhere…" His words cut off when an older woman with her gray hair back in a strict bun stepped out of her condo.

"Evening, Jared."

"Mrs. Maple, I'd like you to meet Wynn Diamond. Wynn, Mrs. Maple. She's a fabulous cook, and before you stepped into my life she always made sure I was fed."

She offered her free hand to the older woman. "It's nice to meet you, Mrs. Maple."

"Please call me Lilian." She lightly shook Wynn's hand before letting it go. "I hope you're feeding him more than just cupcakes. That boy has a nasty sweet tooth, but he needs real nourishment."

As if her words reminded him of the cupcakes, he reached for the box again, easing the lid open. She sidestepped, keeping the cupcakes just out of his grasp. "Don't worry, I'm making him lunch before he's allowed to touch these."

"Good." She nodded. "I'll see you again soon. Right now, I must be on my way to an appointment. You take care of him, you hear?"

"It was nice to meet you, and don't worry about Jared. He's in good hands."

"No doubt, child, no doubt." Mrs. Maple laughed as she continued past them.

While he opened the door to his condo, she leaned close. "You have her wrapped around your finger, don't you? Letting her bring you food when you know damn well you can cook."

"But she's a better cook than I am." He pushed the door open. "Give me ten minutes. I want to shower and change, then I'm all yours."

"I'll get lunch together. We'll eat here before we head out on the water." She tossed her overnight bag by the door before she forced herself toward the kitchen, when all she wanted to do was follow him into the bedroom.

Since he showed up in her life, she was making up for all the sex-free months. Her desires ran deeper than ever before, controlling her actions, instead of the other way around. If she wasn't working, she was thinking about him. Not all her thoughts ran sexual, but they all contained him. He was her drug; she always wanted him around. How she would handle it when he had to deploy, she wasn't sure, but she was committed. If the times they had together were always like this then she'd find a way to make it work. Thick or thin, he was hers.

With the sandwiches made and sitting on the table, she glanced at the clock. Ten minutes had passed since the water had shut off. What was taking him so long? "Boom?" She strolled back to the bedroom, expecting to see him spread out on the bed naked and waiting for her.

"I'll make arrangements." He sat on the bed and with a trembling hand rubbed his eyebrows. "I'll be in touch soon." He ended the call and tossed the phone on the bed.

"Babe, what is it?" She went and knelt down in front of him, her hands on his forearms. The tight muscles under her fingers told her there was anger heating within him. "Jared, look at me."

Seconds ticked by until he finally did what she asked, yet he remained silent. "Please tell me what's wrong. If it's a deployment, we'll reschedule our weekend. Things will be fine." The words left her mouth and fear spiked within her. Their first deployment together…she knew what to expect from Ace and Lucky's, but being the girlfriend instead of the sister changed things a little.

"Not a deployment." He tried to push her to the side so he could stand but she held on tight as he rose. "My fucking family."

"Whatever it is, we'll deal with it *together*," she reassured him.

"I'm not dragging you into their drama." That shook her enough for him to sidestep her and move to the window.

"Not dragging me into it? I thought we were in this together. You've dealt with my shit, put up with Ace, and now you're going to push me away?" She was no longer afraid, only angry. He was pushing her away without even telling her why.

Refusing to go to him, she rose to sit on the bed. When she looked into his eyes she could see pain, but she refused to force herself in where she wasn't wanted. She'd let him digest whatever the call was about and when he was ready he'd tell her. At least that's what she kept telling herself when all she wanted to do was scream.

Chapter Ten

The first bit of turbulence had hit their relationship in spades and Boom unconsciously tried to push her away. It didn't matter that he did it for a valid reason, it still hurt her just the same. His family was so screwed up he didn't want anyone else to have to deal with that, not if he could help it.

"Damn it." He dragged his hand over his buzz cut. "That's not what I meant."

"Then what did you mean?" She kept her tone hard, hiding her emotions.

"The call was from my mother." He clenched his fist, just thinking about the call made him angry. "My father was in a car accident…it's bad."

"I'm sorry." She shot off the bed, came to him and pressed her body against his, holding him tight.

"I've got to go to them. I'm sorry. Our weekend will have to be rescheduled." He ran his hands up her back, needing to feel her against him while he gathered the strength to deal with the curse he called family.

"Don't worry about the weekend, we'll do it later. Your family is more important."

"No, sweet cheeks, you're wrong there. You're more important." He kissed the top of her head. "They're an obligation I must deal with. It's worse than a deployment, at least then I know what I'm getting into. My family is a whole different can of worms."

"We'll get through it. I'll be right by your side."

Every muscle in his body went stiff. "No. You'll stay here."

"What?" She looked up at him, her eyes filled with uncertainties. "I thought you'd want my support."

"I do, but not there. You don't understand my family or what you'd be getting into."

"I don't care about them. I want to be there for you. What's wrong with that?"

"You'll have to deal with their hatred toward me. I had planned for you to *never* have to deal with them." His mother's cruel tongue had already been wagging enough on the phone, degrading him. He didn't want her to have to deal with that.

"I want to be there for you." She ran her hand up his chest. "You have no idea what you're about to walk into or if your father will make it. If you're going home to a hostile environment then you need me. If you're worried things will change between us because of your family, don't be. They have nothing to do with what's between us."

"You have no idea what you'd be walking into. They won't curb their hostility just because you're there. It could be worse and I have no doubt that they will try to take some of it out on you. You shouldn't have to deal with that."

"I'd walk through fire for you, aggression from your family is nothing compared to that." She ran her finger over his cheek. "Where are we heading?"

"Minneapolis." Saying his hometown sent dread through him. He didn't want to go there or see his family. Though if his father was actually dying, as his mother claimed, then it was his duty. *Fourteen years.*

"Guess that means I should make plane reservations while you pack. If we have time I need to go to my condo and grab a few other things before we leave." She rose up onto her tiptoes and pressed a kiss to his lips.

"I'm going to owe you big for this." He hugged her tight, not willing to let her go yet. "Leave the dates open, we'll fly back as soon as we know how my father is. If he'll live we'll be on a plane back tonight."

"However long you'll need," she reassured him. "Where's your laptop? I left mine at home."

"On the coffee table in the living room, my credit card is in my wallet." He nodded at the dresser, trying to get his thoughts in order.

"I'll deal with it. Are you okay?"

"Going home after fourteen long years of having little to no contact with any of them makes me sick." He leaned his head back against the wall, making a solid thump as it connected. "One of the men on the team said going home always makes him feel like a child again, but for me it's sickening. They call and I jump, even after all they've said and all I know they'll do when I arrive."

"You go because even through all the shit they've put you through, you still care about them. I'll apologize for saying this upfront, but everything you told me about your parents…they're assholes and don't deserve shit from you, yet I support you going because I would do the same in your case. You're better than them and this shows it." She cupped the sides of his face and their gazes met. "This right here, how you feel…it's only going to get worse when you arrive. That is why I'm going with you."

"I don't deserve you." He hugged her tight to him, lifting her slightly off the ground.

"Don't think this won't cost you," she teased. "I still want that boat trip out to the middle of the water where you're going to make love to me under the stars, just like you promised."

"When this is done I'll do that and so much more." When she started to move away to go make the reservations he pulled her back until she was pressed against him. "Wynn…I love you." He had felt it for a while now, but had kept it to himself so he wouldn't scare her away, at that moment it just felt right.

"Oh, Jared." She wrapped her arms around his neck, bringing their faces as close as their height difference would allow. "I never thought I could feel like this, but I love you."

Her declaration gave him the courage he needed to face his family. It was funny, but fighting terrorists was easier than going up against his family and their disapproval. With her by his side, he'd take them and the world on single-handedly. *Watch out, here we come...*

Capturing a Diamond – SEALed for You

Chapter Eleven

A cool breeze cut through the air, spraying a white powder mist of snow into the air from one of the many piles still littering the area. While the weather had just begun to turn cold in Virginia, it was already cold and occasionally snowy in Minnesota. There was nothing there that Boom missed, his hometown had too many skeletons that needed to stay in his past.

"Miss Diamond?" A man in a suit came toward them, his hand outstretched.

"That's me." She accepted his hand. "The car?"

"Right there, just as you requested." He danged the keys in front of her. "If you should require anything else…"

"I'll let you know, thank you." She looked back at Jared, who remained silent. "If you're ready?"

"As ready as I will be." He laid his free arm at the small of her back as they made their way to the sleek black car that waited for them. "Do I even want to know how you managed to do that and avoid the rental car agencies?"

"His brother has a shop in the Mall of America, and I do custom work for it occasionally. I made a deal with him if he could have a car waiting for me outside the airport. I figured it would save time. He also has a rental apartment downtown that we'll be staying at, it will allow us to avoid a hotel and have some privacy."

"You shouldn't have had to call in favors on my behalf." He tossed their bags into the trunk.

"Don't." She leaned into him. "It was nothing and allowed us to get out of here quickly. You still have time to see your father before visiting hours are over."

"How did I get so lucky?" he whispered, his lips hovering just above hers.

"I'm the lucky one." She closed the distance, pressing their lips together, and set the keys in his hand. "You drive; you know where we're going."

"How about we go to the apartment instead?" The apartment sounded good, but what sounded better was going back into the airport and catching the first flight back to Virginia. He didn't want to be here or deal with this family shit.

"That's your choice, but we came here to see how your father is doing. If you put it off it's only going to make you more anxious than you are now."

"Okay. Let's get this over with then we'll find a quiet place to get something to eat." He opened her door for her before going around the other side of the car and getting behind the wheel. "I hope you're ready to visit hell on earth, because that's what it will be like."

"Maybe your mom will be more concerned about your father and it won't be so bad." Her voice held a tone of optimism.

"Not a chance. I've already had her spew venom at me on the phone, it will be worse in person." He wondered again why he felt any obligation to his family; after all, they never felt anything for him. It had been fourteen years since he signed the papers to join the Navy, which was the turning point in his family dynamics. Any anger he received as a child from his parents when he didn't do what they wanted him to do was nothing compared to what was unleashed the day he told them he joined the military.

She gently caressed his leg, pulling him back to reality. "You're doing the right thing."

"I hope so." He glanced in the side mirror until it was finally clear and he could pull out of the loading zone. The famous line, *you can never go home again* ran through his mind. Very true in his case, he had made his decision and the consequences be damned.

Wynn left her hand on Boom's leg, giving him what comfort she had to offer as she stared out the window, taking in Minnesota as he remained silent beside her. The last few hours had been tense and she just kept hoping it wouldn't be as bad as he thought it would be. Not for her sake, because she didn't care what they thought of her coming with him, but for his. Despite all his family's faults, he still cared for them even if they refused to accept his life and career.

She was there to give him the support he needed, to help in any way, and she'd do what she could to keep the family drama at bay. Hopefully then he could focus on his father, instead of flinging venom with the rest of his family. She expected his mother to be an issue, but the wildcard in all of it was his younger brother. In fourteen years they had barely spoken, so neither of them were sure how that would go. Maybe it would be the calming point of this whole mess, or maybe he'd been brainwashed by their parents' hatred and things would be worse.

Her plan was to be supportive and, not wanting to make things worse for him, she'd try to keep her mouth shut when it came to drama. With that in mind, she also knew there would only be so much she could take. She loved him and that wouldn't allow her to stand by idly while someone tore him to shreds, no matter who it was. Maybe it was the Diamond family trait coming out in her. None of them could stand by while someone was being hurt. Plus, she understood what it was like to have someone not respect your choices. Things weren't this bad for her and she never thought it would be the case, but if things were reversed she hoped he'd back her.

"I'm not very good company, but you're being awful quiet." He laid his hand over hers.

"It's fine. I was giving you time to get yourself mentally prepared."

"I'm as prepared as I'll be, plus, that's the hospital." He tipped his head forward to the large brick building as he pulled into the turn off. "Ready or not…"

She swallowed the lump that formed in her throat and nodded. "I'm ready, but I don't know about you."

He pulled into a parking spot and shut the car off. "I should have forced you to stay home but my own greed wanted you here by my side."

"I'm a grown woman and I wanted to come. You couldn't have forced me to do anything. Now let's go, you only have forty minutes until visiting hours are over." She opened her door and stepped out of the car, hoping he'd do the same because she didn't want to drag him out.

"You're worse than Ace," he bitched as he came around the car.

"It's a Diamond trait." She slipped her arm around his waist, letting her fingers travel under his shirt for skin contact. "You're here for your father. Try to ignore everything else, and let their attitudes fall where they may because they don't change who we are or what's between us."

"That's easier said than done."

"I know." They made their way across the hospital parking lot, but before they could enter the front door, she tugged on the belt loop of his jeans, bringing them to a halt. "Before we go in…I just wanted to let you know I love you."

She wasn't sure those three little words would help, but something inside her told her that he needed to hear it. It would remind him someone was in his corner, watching his back. Just as she had Ace and Lucky to help her when their parents got out of hand, she'd be there to do the same for him. They were a team. One that understood the power words held but wouldn't let that defeat them from their goals and aspirations.

Chapter Twelve

The awful stench of illness and bleach enveloped Boom as they stepped through the main doors, stealing the breath from his lungs. Hospitals were the one place he always hated. The stench never seemed to disappear, and hidden within the walls were people breathing their last. With his career death was always a possibility, one that he didn't want to think about, but being in hospitals always brought that to the forefront of his mind. How many brothers and sisters in arms did he see die over the last fourteen years? Too many.

"Thirty-one hours after the accident and you finally have the nerve to show up." Hatred slashed out like a whip.

"Aunt Cindy." He laced his fingers through Wynn's and stepped closer to his aunt, trying to keep their conversation from being overheard by everyone in the lobby. "My mother called me this morning and I boarded the first flight I could. How is he?"

"He's dying and his eldest son isn't at his bedside. How do you think he's doing?"

"I'm here now. Are Mom and Justin with him?"

"Yeah. I see you brought your flag chaser with you as well." If the look his aunt gave Wynn could have killed, she'd have been dead before he could stop it.

"Wynn is kind enough to accompany me home and I won't stand for comments like that." He glared at his aunt, unwilling to let her intimidate him. "Come along, sweetie, time is short."

With their hands still laced together, he led the way to the elevator, ignoring the people that stared after overhearing the conversation. "I'm sorry."

"If that's as bad as it will be, then this will be a piece of cake." She tried to make light of the situation as the elevator doors closed and he wrapped his arms around her.

"Oh sweet cheeks, that's just the beginning. Aunt Cindy is my father's sister, but she's not nearly as bad as my father or even my mother." The elevator crept to a stop and he laid a gentle kiss on the top of her head. "I'm sorry for what she said."

"Flag chaser? Who cares? I love you, not the uniform you wear, you know that and that's what matters."

He nodded. "I remember that uniform is what almost scared you off." The doors opened, revealing the ICU wing, and he let his hands fall away from her. "Here we go."

As they stepped off, she slid her hand back into his. "Within an hour, we'll be at the apartment downtown with a cold beer in hand."

"You make it sound like it's all worth it because there's a beer with our names on it." He tipped his head to smirk at her when he saw his mother step out of a room halfway down the hall. "Here goes nothing."

Drop him in the middle of a gunfight without any weapons and he wouldn't have been as terrified as he was now. Seeing his mother after all these years made him feel like the young kid of only eighteen who had just left home. He hated that she still had that effect on him.

"Jared." She nodded as they neared, eyeing Wynn.

"It's good to see you, Mom. How is he?"

Ignoring the question, she stared at Wynn. "You're not going to introduce us?"

"This is Wynn. Wynn, my mother Karen."

"It's nice to meet you Mrs. Taylor; however, I wish it was under better circumstances."

"I'd have preferred never to meet whatever whore he's with now." She glared at him, hatred in her eyes.

"She's my fiancée, and you'll have respect for her or we'll leave." He let her hand go and wrapped his arm around her shoulders. "I've put up with the insults when they're directed at me, but I will not allow you to berate her."

"Then you shouldn't have brought her here."

"Mom, I'll only ask you once." He stared at her, hoping that she understood that he was serious. He'd leave instead of put Wynn through the torments he had to deal with. "How is Dad?"

"It's bad. They will be taking him in for another surgery within the hour. It's dangerous to do it, but if they don't he won't make it through the night."

"What are the risks with the surgery?"

"It's a seventy-five percent chance he'll die on the table." Tears welled in his mother's eyes, the first sign of weakness he ever saw from her. "He's in and out of consciousness but if you want to see him, go ahead. I'm going to get some coffee at the end of the hall."

"I feel like all I'm doing is apologizing," he whispered once they were alone.

"Fiancée?"

"I'm sorry, it just…I hoped she'd lay off of you then." He rubbed her arm. "I'll tell her the truth."

She shook her head, her hair brushing against his arm. "It will only make things worse. Let's see how he's doing."

They stepped into the room and the sickly copper scent of blood filled the air. His father lay in the middle of the bed, tubes rubbing here and there, and all he felt was regret. Regret that his father couldn't accept who he was or what he wanted to do. For most families, having a child join the military was a sense of pride, there was fear of what might happen mixed in, but never hatred. His parents didn't believe in violence unless it was coming from them. His father had a mean right hook and a worse backhand, and more times than he cared to remember was he on the receiving side of those.

He looked down at his father. The strong man had never been sick as long as Boom had known him and now he lay in the middle of the hospital bed as white as the sheet that covered him. Black and blue marks covered his face and arms, one eye was completely shut from the swelling, and his left arm was in a full cast. Seeing the injuries and knowing that most of the damage was done internally, he was surprised his father was still alive.

"I don't want you here!" His father's angry words cut through his thoughts, and he looked up to find the man glaring at him.

"Mom called."

"I don't care. Don't come crawling back now. You've made it clear over the years that the military is more important than your family."

"Damn it, Dad." He bit his tongue to keep from rehashing the same thing with his father. "I came because of the accident. We're family. This is no time for this childish hatred."

"We're not family. You deserted your family fourteen years ago." A cough racked his body until he spit blood into the spit pan. "I only have one son and Justin is on duty."

Duty? He had a brief moment to wonder what career they forced his younger brother into before his mother walked into the room.

"Get out! Take your flag-chasing whore with you. I don't want you here. You're dead to me!" his father raged.

"What's going on here, Mr. Taylor?" A woman in pale blue scrubs stepped into the room. "You know you can't get upset in your condition."

"Get him out of here!" Another coughing fit took control of his father. "He's no son of mine! I want him gone!"

"Sir..." The nurse glanced between them. He suspected she'd ask him to leave but his mother cut her off.

"I shouldn't have called you. It was against his wishes but if..." She paused and it was clear she was going to say if he died.

"It's okay, Mom. He hasn't wanted me around for years. Why should it change when he's dying?" With one last glance at his father, he turned to Wynn. "Let's go."

It sickened him to know that was it, the last tie to his family. No longer would he come somewhere that he wasn't wanted. He made the trip because even after everything they were family, but to be shut out and have Wynn degraded was enough for him to cut any remaining ties. People could think what they wanted, but he could only take so much, and this last bit had been enough.

Chapter Thirteen

Boom stepped into the hall, a mixture of fury and grief pouring through him. The choice he made to join the military was one he never regretted, even with all it cost him over the years: the newest being all family ties. Sure, he hadn't had much family connection since he left for boot camp, but there was still a shimmer of hope that someday things might change. Today proved that would never happen and he grieved for the lost chance.

"Wait, love." Wynn tugged him against the wall, out of the way of the nursing staff going to and from the rooms.

"What?" he snapped before he could rein in his temper. "I'm sorry." He leaned down, pressing their foreheads together.

"We've come all this way. Do you want to find a waiting room and wait to see how the surgery goes?"

"Excuse me…" The nurse from his father's room came toward them. "Mr. Taylor's condition is too grave for any type of excitement.

I'm going to have to ask you to leave, if he's willing to see you, then you may try another visit tomorrow."

"We weren't planning on going back in and you won't have to worry about me upsetting him again. I won't be back. I was just hoping to catch my brother before I left."

"You don't mean Mr. Taylor's son, Doctor Taylor?"

Doctor Taylor? He tried to keep the surprise hidden, not to let the nurse know how disconnected he was from his family. "Ummm…I guess I do. Have you seen him?"

The nurse shook her head. "He's on duty in the emergency department, but he was here earlier. If you take the elevator to the first floor and instead of making a right to go back to the main entrance, take a left and at the end of the hall you'll see the sign for the ER."

"Thank you." He glanced down the hall toward his father's room. "Could you see that Mrs. Taylor doesn't forget about her own needs? Make sure she eats something at least."

"I'll do my best, but she hasn't left her husband's side except to get coffee."

He reached into his pocket and pulled out a twenty. "She won't take it from me, but on your break could you grab her a sandwich?"

"Sure." She pocketed the money and stepped away.

"Doctor?" Wynn whispered as they made their way to the elevator.

"It would seem that my father got his way. He pressed me to go to college and become a doctor, but a job like that never held any appeal to me. I don't want to be cooped up indoors, and I never could stand hospitals."

Only thirty and his brother was a doctor. He couldn't believe it. So much had changed over the years, but good or bad he needed to see where things stood between Justin and him before he returned to Virginia. "Looks like we can catch a flight home in the morning and we'll still have a little time together."

"Maybe things will change once they have time to think about it." She squeezed his hand.

"No." The elevator doors closed, giving them a moment alone as they traveled to the first floor. "Those doors have closed. It's time for me to grieve for my family and move on with our life."

"You know you'll always be a part of the Diamond family." She wrapped her arms around his waist, hugging him.

"I know, and your family is amazing, but I want you." The doors opened before she could say anything else. "Let's see about my brother and then get something to eat."

She opened her mouth as to say something but stopped as a tall lanky man neared them in a white doctor's coat. "Is that…"

"Justin?" It was more of a question to the man than to her.

"Excuse me, do I know you?

"Are you Justin Taylor?" He wanted to make sure, because after fourteen years Justin would have changed.

"Yes. Now who are you?" Justin looked between them, confusion knitting the lines of his face.

"It's me, Jared." He watched his brother carefully, trying to use his training to detect the slightest change in his brother's features.

"Jared." His eyes widened his mouth slack with surprise. "Holy shit, it's been too long. You heard about Dad then?"

"Too long and yeah. I was just up there, but he doesn't want to see me."

"I suspected he wouldn't. What made you come?" Justin stepped to the side to allow others to get on the elevator.

"Mom called." When Justin's gaze traveled to Wynn, he made the same introductions as before. "Justin, this is my fiancée, Wynn."

He held out his hand. "It's nice to meet you."

"You too. I just wish it was under better circumstances." She took his hand, giving it a solid shake.

"I get that Mom called but why come home after all these years?" Justin's gaze left Wynn's and moved to size up Boom.

"Dad's dying; how could I stay away?"

"You've managed to do so up until now."

"When I first left for boot camp I used to call home, write letters, and even try to visit on leave, but every way I tried, I was rejected. They hung up whenever I called, my letters were returned to sender unopened, and they refused to allow me in when I would come back to town. How long did you really think I'd put up with that treatment before I quit trying?" Boom was disappointed that the hatred their parents felt toward him had infected his brother.

"Now that he doesn't want to see you, you'll what? Return home?" Justin shoved his hands into the pockets of his coat and glared at Boom.

"What do you want me to do? Sit around the hospital waiting for some news? Force myself into his room, even after the hospital staff asked me to leave because the patient was getting upset?"

"You shouldn't have even come."

"That's painfully clear now." Boom nodded.

"Stop this." Wynn interrupted. "You're brothers and you have your differences, but this is not the time for this."

"What do you know of it?" Justin glanced at her out of the corner of his eye, keeping his focus on Boom.

"I know enough to see that this hatred is pointless. Every child must grow up, pursue their own life, and choice of career. Jared had the will to do what he wanted no matter the cost, and it's something he has to carry with him for the rest of his life. He dropped everything to come here, even though he knew he'd most likely be rejected. That takes even more courage." She squeezed his hand before continuing. "Right now your father is upstairs dying, so how about everyone puts this hatred aside and focuses on that?"

Justin's beeper blared through the silence that settled over them. "I've got to get back to the ER."

"Dad's having surgery. Could you call and let me know how it goes?"

"What's your number?"

Wynn tugged a piece of paper and pen out of her purse before jotting the information down. "Here. This is his cell number and the address where we're staying. If you change your attitude and want to see him, you're more than welcome to come by."

"Don't count on it." Justin shoved the paper in his pocket and turned on his heels.

"What did I really expect?" Jared mumbled to himself, watching his brother walk down the hall.

"You okay?" She rubbed his arm.

"I'm fine. I didn't except anyone to be happy to see me, but there had been a glimmer of hope that Justin wasn't contaminated by the same hatred my parents had for me." He looked down at her and knew that all that he did in his life brought him to her and that was what mattered. *I wouldn't change a thing.*

Chapter Fourteen

The cool night air didn't soothe Boom's thoughts as he stood on the balcony, looking out at the lights of Minneapolis. It was stupid to come, to think he'd be welcomed, even after his mother had called. The years had proven to be a divider, one that they couldn't destroy now, one that would always be there. His only hope for the whole trip was that it might prove to be the opening he needed to gain back the friendship he had once with Justin, but even that was shattered.

"Can't sleep?" He turned to find Wynn leaning on the glass door, a blanket wrapped around her, blonde hair slightly tousled from sleep. "It's late. You need to get some rest." She came to stand next to him. "How long have you been awake?"

He glanced down, his hands itching to touch her. Awake? Heck, he never got to sleep. After a quiet dinner at a restaurant around the corner, they made their way to the apartment, exhausted. He had gone to bed with her, hoping that cuddling her tight against his body would ease the tension in his body. After hours of lying there staring at the walls, he finally got up.

The smell of sweet vanilla from her shampoo and the round curves of her body hardened his shaft as soon as she settled against his body. "A bit," he lied, not wanting to explain how he'd spent the night.

"Anything I can do to ease the worries on your mind?" She slid her arm across his back, the blanket now wrapped around them both.

"There's nothing we can do here, but I don't want to leave yet."

"Melody will cover the shop, and you've got leave from the SEALs to deal with the family emergency. We'll stay as long as you want."

Her hand caressing his back broke the last of his control. He wrapped his arms around her, pulling her to him, and lowered his head. Their lips met, her mouth opening, letting his tongue explore. His hand slipped under the blanket, grabbing her ass to lift her off her feet. She wrapped her legs around his waist, her arms locked around his neck to draw him closer.

His groin throbbed with desire. He wanted nothing more than to take her to bed and have her scream his name. He broke the kiss, enjoying her warm breath over his face. "I should have left you here while I dealt with my fucked up family."

"Why? Ashamed of me?" Her breath came in gasps.

"Hell no! I just didn't want you to have to deal with their shit, though I have to say it was mild, guess that was because we were in public." He squeezed her tighter to him. "You know, I've wanted you since I first laid eyes on you. I don't think I've ever wanted to be with someone as much as I want you." Adrenaline flooded his veins.

"I want your hands on my body, your lips on mine. Please…" she begged.

Without further invitation, he walked the two quick strides through the door and back to the bedroom. He lowered her on the bed, the blanket discarded on the floor. Whisking her nightshirt over her head, he took in the sight of her naked body. He tossed the nightshirt aside, slid his hand over her waist, and knelt before her. He wedged his body between her legs. Trailing kisses along her neck, hunger coursed through him. He wanted to take his time, get reacquainted with every inch of her body. He claimed her nipple with his mouth, sucking it and flicking his tongue over them.

"Oh, Jared," she moaned, and tugged at his jeans.

Reluctantly, he released her nipple to lay kisses over her shoulder and up her neck until he could gaze into her hazel eyes. "You're beautiful." Her cheeks reddened as he pushed her back on the bed and crawled next to her. "I want you on top, to see your body riding mine. I want to see your beauty highlighted by the moonlight." He rolled onto his back, pulling her with him until she rested on top, caressing her curves.

He slid his hand between their bodies, his fingers teasing her and entering her, tantalizing her with yearning for more. She arched her back, giving his fingers deeper access. As the moonlight accentuated her body, she rode his fingers to orgasm.

"Please, I need you."

He moved his hands to her hips and lifted her. "Up." When she hovered above him, he adjusted so his shaft stood just below her entry. She slowly lowered down. Filling her inch by inch, he pushed her up with her hips before entering her completely. Steadily, his hands on her hips guided their pace.

He leaned forward, locking his mouth on her nipple and sucked until she moaned in pleasure. Her hips increased their pace, driving him forcefully into her with each pump. His thrusts became deeper and faster into a perfect rhythm. They moved together with precision, as if in a well-choreographed dance.

Her body tightened around his shaft and her nails dug into his chest. "Oh, Jared!" she cried out as his own release followed.

Breathless, he brushed her hair from her face. He wanted to see her. Wynn's eyes were glossy and dreamy——the aftermath of amazing sex. She slid off him to lie next to him and snuggle against his body. Content, he pulled the sheet over them, and he lay cradling her, caressing her spine with long, lazy strokes.

"I'm sorry things didn't go better." Her fingers rubbed small circles down his chest.

He kissed the top of her head. "Me too, but it doesn't matter."

She glanced up at him. "Don't lie to me. It does matter to you."

She was right. It did matter, but he learned a long time ago he couldn't change them. "I'm putting it behind me and starting fresh." She gave him a fresh perspective and love of life again. He wasn't going to let it slip through his fingers.

Dawn peeked over the buildings, casting a warm glow across the floor and edge of the bed from where they didn't close the curtains around balcony door. Sleep barely touched Jared through the night, and when it did, it left him with dreams of his family. Being back in his hometown brought everything to the surface. He wanted to return to Virginia, to get away from the memories that were haunting him, but he needed to stick around to see what happened with his father.

She yawned. "The time change is playing with your sleep schedule. You barely slept. Maybe we should close the curtains and stay in bed. There's nothing waiting for us anyways." She curled up in his arms, her left leg and arm draped over him, cuddling close.

"That sounds like the best plan I've heard in the last twenty-four hours. Lift up and I'll get the curtains." He slipped out of bed and padded naked toward the curtains. There was nothing waiting for them to get up, so why not stay in bed cuddled together? She had been his rock through it all and snuggling with her sounded like the perfect way to spend the day.

The doorbell rang, cutting through the stillness of the morning. "Fuck!"

"I guess that ends our quiet morning before it even starts." She sat up, grabbing the silk robe that she had tossed at the edge of the bed the night before.

"Who knows we're here?"

"Besides my friend who owns the apartment? Only your brother and my friend wouldn't stop by."

"Fuck."

"Is that going to be your word of the day?" She tied the robe. "Get dressed. I'll answer the door."

"No, you've dealt with enough of their shit." He grabbed the shorts he started the night in and cut off her access to the door. "I'll deal with him."

"*We* will, remember, we're a team."

"What would I do without you by my side?" He kissed her quickly and strolled hand-in-hand with her to the door. "Here goes nothing." Facing a terrorist behind the door would have held less stress than the idea of his brother, or any of his family being on the other side. Too bad he couldn't just shoot them and be done with it, like he could in the midst of a battle.

Chapter Fifteen

Jared tugged the door open and there stood a very disheveled Justin, his eyes red-rimmed. His stomach sank with the knowledge that there was only one thing that would bring Justin here in that condition. He stepped aside, letting his brother in.

"I programmed the coffee pot before we went to bed. It should be ready." Wynn rushed off to the kitchen.

"Have a seat, Justin." He nodded to the small living area.

"He's…" Justin started, but stopped when Wynn returned with the coffee.

"Here, drink this." She handed him a mug before going to perch on the arm of the chair next to Boom.

Justin took a sip of the coffee before setting it aside. "Dad never made it off the table and died early this morning."

The announcement did nothing for Boom. He had expected loss to set in but there was nothing. No sadness, no loss, just nothing.

Years ago, he had grieved for the loss of his family, so this didn't change anything. You couldn't grieve again for someone who had been out of your life for fourteen years.

"You have nothing to say?"

"What would you like me to say, Justin? Dad, Mom and you have been out of my life for too long. I don't know the man who died today. By all means, he was a complete stranger. Do you grieve for someone who came into the emergency room? No, because you didn't know them. You do your job and try to save them, but you don't grieve for each person."

"He's your father, not a stranger."

"Justin, I really don't want to get into this with you." Wynn rubbed a small circle on his back to keep him in his chair instead of pacing the floor.

"It doesn't matter." Justin rubbed his eyes, looking back at him. "Mom wishes to respect Dad's final wishes and doesn't want you at the funeral."

"Fine. We'll be leaving soon, so there's nothing to worry about." He swallowed fury. "If that's the only reason you've come then you can leave."

"I just wanted to inform you of our father's demise." Justin stood and walked to the door. "You joined the military and that was the end of things for you, while I had to stay home and deal with our parents. You got off easy."

"You only had a year and a half until you were eighteen and then you could have done whatever you wanted." Boom didn't turn around; he didn't need to see any of the hatred on his brother's face.

"I didn't have the courage you did. All your life you went against the grain, doing things your way instead of Dad's, while I worked twice as hard to make it up to him. It's why I went into medicine. I thought it would please him, but nothing was ever good enough for Dad."

"If you don't enjoy medicine, get out of it." Boom turned in his chair to look behind him. "It's your life and when it comes down to it, you have to make sure you're happy. You have to live with your life choices, not Mom and Dad."

"Yeah we do, and look where yours got you."

"Yes, look at where mine got me." He stood up and pulled Wynn into his embrace. "I've got a career I enjoy and I woman I love more than life itself. I couldn't have asked for a better outcome."

Justin glared at them for a moment, but there wasn't just hatred reflecting in his eyes, there was also jealousy. Before Boom could comment, Justin left without another word, slamming the door behind him.

"Oh Jared, I'm sorry."

"Marry me."

She leaned away from their embrace to look at him. "What?"

"Marry me." He cupped her hand into his, bought it to his lips, and laid a kiss on her knuckle. "What I said to Justin just now is true. You are my rock. You've put up with the shit my family flung and didn't even bat an eye. I love you more than I ever thought possible and I want to spend the rest of my life with you."

"Do you realize this is crazy?"

"Yes, but we've both always done the crazy stuff. I'm not asking that you marry me tomorrow, but I want you as my wife."

"Jared Taylor, you're all I think about from the time I wake up until I go to sleep. Even in my dreams, you play a constant part. I couldn't imagine my life without you. Yes, I'll marry you."

He kissed her, long and sensual, claiming her as his again. When their lips finally parted he whispered, "Who's going to break it to Ace?"

"That's all you." She laid her hand on his chest. "It's time for you to live up to your famous nickname and deal with the explosion also known as my brother."

"I wonder if I just got the short end of this deal," he teased.

She kissed him again. "I need to shower." She untied the robe and let it fall to the floor.

"I'll lock the door and then I'm going to join you." Watching her pad naked to the bathroom caused his shaft to harden with desire. Images of the soapy water cascading down her silky body had him quickly checking the locks before dashing after her.

In the bathroom, he could see the outline of her body in the fogged glass door. He stripped off his shorts, tossed them on the sink, and opened the door to join her. Steam billowed out of the shower. The heat of the shower called to his tense muscles, he wanted it as much as he wanted her. She leaned against the blue and white glass mosaic tiles, the showerhead spraying water down her naked body, sending soap bubbles rushing toward the drain.

"Damn, you're even more beautiful wet."

"You've already had me wet." She winked at him.

"I plan to do it again, right now." For a moment, he stood there enjoying the way the soap bubbles slid over her body. He gently tugged her arm, pulling her closer to him, and in one quick motion he pushed her gently against the shower wall. Giving in to temptation, he ran his hands up her slippery back.

He crushed his mouth to hers and slid his hand between her legs. Unerringly finding her core, he teased the bundle of nerves and dragged pleasure from her in hard, hot waves. She moaned around his unrelenting kiss. He held her captive against the wall, his fingers thrusting into her as his thumb continued to wring more pleasure from her body. "Jared." She tipped her head back, her nails clawing at shoulders as the tidal wave of orgasm smashed through her.

"Take me," she murmured against his mouth.

His teeth grazed her lower lip and he pulled his hand away. She cried out in frustration, but he ignored her demands. Gripping her hips, he lifted her and spread her thighs before he drove into her with one powerful thrust. He gave her no time to catch her breath before he began rocking in and out of her. She had no control, no say as he left her mouth and kissed a path to her neck. Digging her nails into his shoulders, she held on to him as every thrust of his hips sent pulses of pleasure exploding through her. She came apart at the seams, her inner muscles clenching around him as he continued to drive into her.

He slammed home in a frenzy and his climax burst through as a second orgasm shook her body. He held her tight until her body calmed, his hands on her hips kept her from collapsing into a heap on the shower floor. She was amazing in every way.

Wynn sat on the edge of the bed with her cell phone in her hand and tears splashing down her face when Jared came back from the pub with sandwiches for lunch. The phone call she had been waiting for had finally come in, only it seemed like the wrong time for such news.

"Sweet cheeks, what is it?" He knelt in front of her. "Did something happen?"

"New York…"

"You've finally heard from them? What did they say?" He held her hands in his, rubbing his thumb along her wrist.

"The timing is all wrong." She shook her head.

"Oh sweetie, I'm sorry." He started to get up to sit beside her.

"No, it's not that…they want my designs. It took longer than I expected for them to get back to me. I had almost given up hope, but their delay was because they wanted to offer me a larger contract. A large display and in two different Fifth Avenue shops. The contract has been sent to my office."

"Sweetie, that's wonderful! Why the tears?"

"The timing. I shouldn't be happy and celebrating when you just lost your father." She pulled her hand from his grasp and wiped the tears.

"No, this is perfect timing. I grieved a long time ago for the family I lost. Tonight we'll go celebrate and tomorrow afternoon we'll go back to Virginia. We'll even be on time for the dinner with Ace and Gwen."

"Dinner tonight sounds good, but tomorrow with Ace, maybe we should put it off."

"No way, my beautiful fiancée. We're going to take the bull by the horns and tell Ace of our pending wedding and your newest adventure to New York. Everything is going to be perfect. See, our life is coming together, one step at a time."

"You're amazing, Jared, and I love you." She wasn't sure that everything was going to be perfect but she wasn't going to fight it at the moment. Tomorrow she'd worry about Ace's reaction and what her parents would think of her branching Roll of the Diamond's designs out to New York stores, while tonight she'd celebrate with Jared and let the cards fall where they would.

Capturing a Diamond – SEALed for You

Epilogue

The holiday season was quickly approaching and Wynn was ready for her first holidays with the newest additions: her sister-in-law Gwen, her niece, and most of all her new husband. Thanksgiving was only a week away and her parents would be arriving soon, though she tried not to think about that. Besides her parents still being opposed to her career, maybe now more than ever since she was married, all the other tumbling blocks of life were finally coming together. Finding Jared, Roll of the Diamond was doing better than it ever had, not to mention the expansion to New York being a hit; everything in her life was perfect. Even Ace had accepted her marriage and welcomed Jared into the family with open arms. They'd watch each other's backs during deployments, making sure they both made it home in one piece.

Wynn sat at the dining room table, holding her niece, Roulette. She rocked the sweet little girl in her arms, amazed at all the thick blonde hair she had. She looked more like an Angel with her blonde hair and blue eyes but Ace and Gwen had stuck with the family tradition of naming the kids after the Vegas parties the Diamond family used to host.

"I leave you alone for ten minutes and you're holding her. What happened to her napping?"

"She woke up and demanded her auntie's attention. Didn't you, sweetie?" She looked down at her dozing niece.

"Sure." Gwen set the laundry aside and plopped down on a chair across the table from Wynn.

"Where are our men?"

"I don't know, but I can tell you Ace is on baby duty tonight. I haven't slept more than three hours in the last forty-eight. That beautiful niece of yours has an ear infection and her sleep schedule is off."

She took note of the dark circles shadowing Gwen's eyes. "Jared and I could take her for the night if you want? Then you and Ace can get some sleep."

"Oh no, I'm well aware of that deadline you have with New York. I won't interrupt that with Roulette. You can have her for a long weekend after the newlywed stage, if she isn't in college by then." Gwen laughed at her own smart-ass comment. "Seriously though, I know you need to get the designs sent to New York before the holidays and with your parents arriving Saturday time is limited."

"Things will settle down after the holidays and I promise I'll take her. You and Ace need some quality couple time."

Before Gwen could comment, the front door swung open. "We're home!" Ace called.

"Shhh, my niece is sleeping." She scolded her brother, before seeing Jared come in behind Ace, looking a little green around the gills. "Hey, sweetie. Everything okay?"

"We've received word of training the week after Thanksgiving."

Her heart sank. Training and deployments were part of military life, but since this was their first holiday season today she had hoped he would at least be able to be there through it, especially for Christmas. "Will you be home for Christmas?"

"The training should take two weeks, but we'll be home for Christmas and unless we're called up for a mission we'll be home through the New Year." He laid his hand on her shoulder, giving it a gentle squeeze.

"Good." She rubbed the side of her head against the back of his hand. This would be their first actual training as a married couple where he'd be away, but since they got together she knew they'd make it through it and anything else life threw at them. They were in it through thick and thin. "It will be fine. What about the leave for New York, did you get it approved?"

Jared nodded. "Everything is set for that."

"What's this about New York?" Ace came back in from the kitchen with beers.

"The shops on Fifth Avenue that have been showcasing my work are doing a fashion show after the New Year and some of my work will be included. I need to be there and Jared will be going with me. I will also be meeting with a new shop there about another line I'm launching."

"Another line?" Gwen asked. "How are you going to manage that when you've just purchased the adjoining shop by your boutique to expand?"

"Actually, the boutique isn't expanding, the new line will take over the new shop. We're set to open at the end of January." She reached over and laid her niece back in the bassinet, before grabbing a garment from her purse and handing it to Gwen.

"What is this?" She unfolded the first dress for the line. It was a cute little Navy-inspired dress: a white top with a blue collar and a single line of America flag buttons and a waist that ruffled out into a blue skirt.

"The new line. It started when I wanted to make a few special things for Roulette. Our men inspired that one, along with a few other ones that will only be carried in the Virginia Beach boutique to cater to our military families." She waited for Gwen to look up from the outfit. "Heart of Diamond will be baby and toddler outfits."

"She got the idea when we found out she's expecting." Jared squeezed her hand. "Our son or daughter will be born in June."

"That's wonderful!" Gwen dashed around the table, her arms wrapping around Wynn in a tight hug. "I'm so happy for the both of you and the design is beautiful! I'm sure you'll be a success with the new branch."

She watched Ace over her sister-in-law's shoulder as he sat with his beer. "I wouldn't expect for my nieces or nephews look anything but as if they just walked off the catwalk. You've always had an eye for fashion, not settling for the comfortable jeans and T-shirts most favor. Congratulations."

"Thank you," she whispered as her brother took Gwen's place hugging her.

"Mom's going to…"

With a wave of her hand, she cut off Ace. "Please, I know she's going to have a fit. Our parents believe that I should be a stay at home wife like Mom was, but I can't, not completely. I'll have Melody running Roll of the Diamond and I've been interviewing someone to handle Heart of Diamond, but I'm not stepping back completely. I'll focus on the designs, handle things from home as much as I can, but I won't give up or close the shops." Unable to sit while Ace towered nearby, she stood up from the chair.

"I'm not asking you to, just as I didn't ask Gwen to give up her career. I understand that you both love what you do and that's what matters. It also gives you something to occupy your time with when we're deployed. I just want you to be prepared for what Mom's going to say when she finds out."

"We'll handle your parents." Jared slipped his arm around her waist, pulling her close. "Designing and the boutiques are something she enjoys, it's time your parents start to accept that and be supportive, or keep their mouths shut."

"I couldn't have put it better myself." She leaned up kissing him. "My husband supports me and that's what matters most. It's also nice to have the backing from Lucky, Gwen and you. It gives me the courage to do what I love."

Filled with love, she snuggled against Jared's body. He supported her and loved her through everything, even the long hours she had been putting in recently. All those years she had refused to even consider someone in uniform had finally led her to the perfect man. The one that now had her heart. Everything was perfect. Finally, she got her very own happy ever after...

Marissa Dobson

Born and raised in the Pittsburgh, Pennsylvania area, Marissa Dobson now resides about an hour from Washington, D.C. She's a lady who likes to keep busy, and is always busy doing something. With two different college degrees, she believes you're never done learning.

Being the first daughter to an avid reader, this gave her the advantage of learning to read at a young age. Since learning to read, she has always had her nose in a book. It wasn't until she was a teenager that she started writing down the stories she came up with.

Marissa is blessed with a wonderful supportive husband, Thomas. He's her other half and allows her to stay home and pursue her writing. He puts up with all her quirks and listens to her brainstorm in the middle of the night.

Her writing buddies Max (a cocker spaniel) and Dawne (a beagle mix) are always around to listen to her bounce ideas off them. They might not be able to answer, but they are helpful in their own ways.

She love to hear from readers so send her an email at marissa@marissadobson.com or visit her online at http://www.marissadobson.com.

Capturing a Diamond – SEALed for You

Other Books by Marissa Dobson

Alaskan Tigers Series:

Tiger Time

The Tiger's Heart

Tigress for Two

Night with a Tiger

Trusting a Tiger

Jinx's Mate

Two for Protection

Stormkin Series:

Storm Queen

Reaper Series:

A Touch of Death

SEALed for You Series:

Ace in the Hole

Explosive Passion

Capturing a Diamond

Fate Series:

Snowy Fate

Sarah's Fate

Mason's Fate

As Fate Would Have It

Half Moon Harbor Resort Series:

Learning to Live

Learning What Love Is

Her Cowboy's Heart

Half Moon Harbor Resort Volume One

Clearwater Series:

Winterbloom

Unexpected Forever

Losing to Win

Christmas Countdown

The Surrogate

Clearwater Romance Volume One

Stand Alone:

Secret Valentine

Restoring Love

The Twelve Seductive Days of Christmas

CPSIA information can be obtained at www.ICGtesting.com
Printed in the USA
LVOW07s1629100515

437948LV00001B/139/P